PRAISE FOR THE ⌐

"Lusciously emotional…in this engaging story of fate and adult friendship, Teleky manages that stunning and rare feat – telling an ordinary story of human interaction in a way that is universal, revelatory and suspenseful." —*Globe and Mail*

"Exquisite…A relentless observer of human frailty, Teleky always spies the human gesture." —*National Post*

"A beautifully textured, beautifully structured novel…a book to savour and reflect upon long after you've turned the last page."
—*Vancouver Star*

"Teleky has always been a writer's writer…with *Pack Up the Moon* he delivers an eloquent exploration of the demands and limits of friendship and faith." —*Ottawa Citizen*

"A rare, affecting novel about sorrowing over ghosts…the expert dissection of a human heart." —*Toronto Star*

The
Blue Hour

RICHARD TELEKY

Publishers of Singular
Fiction, Poetry, Nonfiction, Translations and Drama

Library and Archives Canada Cataloguing in Publication

Teleky, Richard, 1946-, author
The blue hour : a novel / Richard Teleky.

Issued in print and electronic formats.
ISBN 978-1-55096-666-4 (softcover).--ISBN 978-1-55096-667-1 (EPUB).--
ISBN 978-1-55096-668-8 (Kindle).--ISBN 978-1-55096-669-5 (PDF)

PS8589.E375B58 2017   C813'.54   C2017-901182-0
                                                C2017-901183-9

Published by Exile Editions Ltd ~ www.ExileEditions.com
144483 Southgate Road 14 – GD, Holstein, Ontario, N0G 2A0
Printed and Bound in Canada by Marquis.

Publisher's note: This is a work of fiction.
Names, characters, places and incidents either are the product
of the author's imagination or are used fictitiously.

We gratefully acknowledge the Canada Council for the Arts,
the Government of Canada, the Ontario Arts Council,
and the Ontario Media Development Corporation
for their support toward our publishing activities.

Conseil des Arts du Canada   Canada Council for the Arts   Canadä

ONTARIO ARTS COUNCIL
CONSEIL DES ARTS DE L'ONTARIO
an Ontario government agency
un organisme du gouvernement de l'Ontario

Ontario
Ontario Media Development
Corporation

Canadian sales representation:
The Canadian Manda Group, 664 Annette Street,
Toronto ON M6S 2C8   www.mandagroup.com   416 516 0911

North American and international distribution, and U.S. sales:
Independent Publishers Group, 814 North Franklin Street,
Chicago IL 60610   www.ipgbook.com   toll free: 1 800 888 4741

For my ghosts

Can a human being, fully aware of the eternity behind and before him or her, fully value and appreciate the passing hour? An hour of watching the woods or the sea or of listening to music, an hour given to friendly talk with friends? —ISAK DINESEN

Prologue

One night last summer, very late, when I couldn't sleep, when I tossed about on my bed, shifting my position every few minutes, plumping my pillow again and again, this thought came to mind: would the same police stretcher that bore a securely-strapped body to the morgue have been used, six weeks later, to carry another body, this one only wounded, to the hospital? Possibly yes, and even likely, in a small town of eight thousand, like ours. It wouldn't have mattered, of course, not to anyone – certainly not to either of them. I won't pretend to feel the smack of my skull against a concrete wall, or ponder whether there's shock before pain in the moment of impact, or question if fading sight turns into panic, nor does an imagined bullet's sharp burn give my mind even the hint of sensation, let alone my flesh. And I can't know if one feels death stalking, then coming forward in the same room, quite brazen, or the relief that it isn't nearby after all. But an odd notion remains with me, and I've kept asking myself, as if a padded metal stretcher has a mind of its own, perhaps some conscious sense of a body's impress and weight, what is remembered?

One

How useful an office one's friends perform when they recall us.
Yet how painful to be recalled, to be mitigated, to have one's self
adulterated, mixed up, become part of another.
                              —VIRGINIA WOOLF, *The Waves*

1

Saturday, March 17, 2012

"We're still passionate," Nick said. "I wouldn't want you to think we aren't. But usually it's just once a month."

People often tell me things I don't need to know.

"And afterward I'm depleted for days," he added. "Élan vital's precious. Some athletes abstain before a big game."

I nodded, and he sighed. Wasn't it King Lear who said, "Let copulation thrive!"? I should look it up.

From the start, let's get this straight. I'm not going to write much about myself. Sure, I have a house, a portable computer, a five-year-old Jetta, but no microwave, no iPod, no cell phone. Get the picture? I also have an old piano, a snow blower, and a job at the college – as a librarian archivist. And I've never cared for mysteries where the detective rambles on about his failed romances or new loves, his fears or obsessions, so there'll be none of that. Death has its way in this story, and in its own time, yet death can wait. For a while, at least, we're safe.

Perhaps the early spring made Nick eager to declare his passions, like a horny young shepherd in a pastoral poem. Long ago I learned that when one part of a couple shares uncalled-for intimacies, or criticizes the other half, you're supposed to keep a blank expression, taking it in benignly but not really remembering; you're not supposed to comment, or agree.

To avoid hearing more, I said, "It's a good doughnut, isn't it?"

He chewed thoughtfully and then replied, "I'm sorry Hedy's running late."

We were sitting outside of Gibson's, at one of the sidewalk tables overlooking the town common, properly known as Tappan Square. It was mid-March but unseasonably warm. Record-breaking, in fact. The bulbs in my garden had already opened, and students were out in T-shirts and skimpy shorts, though St. Patrick's Day usually meant the end of winter in northern Ohio.

I glanced down at the headline of this week's *Oberlin Review* – "Panel On Biometrics" – which seemed safe enough in case Nick noticed it. In the last few years Nick and Hedy had become vocal members of the Tea Party, and our visits were now a minefield. Somewhere I read a Chinese saying that you know you're getting old when you don't see old friends as much as you used to because it takes too much patience. I never thought this would happen, but it has. And the tensions in our friendship have left me troubled, at a loss.

Nick's cell phone rang. He took it from his pocket, smiled, and then put the thing to his ear. "Hello, dear." Perhaps Hedy would be joining us soon.

"No, we're outside," he said, pausing. "Uh-huh, sure. And Mother's feeling better." He mouthed "Guy" to me and I turned away.

Guy, poor sad Guy, their only child – thirty-four, and finally moving into his own place.

Should I buy a second doughnut? If you're ever in Oberlin, try a whole-wheat fried cake, they're one of the first things alumni head for when they return to campus on the nostalgia trail. Since 1885, Gibson's candy-*cum*-general store has been on the same spot on West College Street, and now it's a local landmark.

"We'll see you tonight," I heard Nick say. Then, "Yes, yes. I love you. See you later."

"He's really doing it?" I asked.

Guy had rented a bungalow in town, an hour's drive from his parents' place in Medina. They'd been talking about his search for a year now, but I didn't think he had the nerve.

"We're happy for him, setting out on his own like this. The economy's been hard on young people." He sighed, with the hint of a rueful smile. "We're finally empty nesters."

"What's wrong, Nick? You don't sound pleased."

"I guess you never really expect big changes. And Hedy's worried about him."

"Mothers are like that," I commiserated. "He'll be fine."

Another thing I've learned is that couples with children want the freedom to criticize their kids but you aren't supposed to join in. Best, in fact, to mount their defense. Yet when it came to Guy, I had no idea what to say. I hadn't known him as a child, I was then working in Canada, and he'd been a quiet teenager, never making a fuss. Unexpectedly, he joined the army right out of high school, but after his stint returned home, did odd jobs, and finally trained as a dental tech. He continued to live with his parents and help with their antiques business. People used to say that a happy marriage bred old maids, and Guy was fast becoming one.

"We've had a theft in the archives," I said, hoping to distract Nick. "Part of a rare map."

"Important?" Nick feigned interest.

"It can't be replaced. People think archives are dull, but a cut from a razor blade..."

"Hey, fellas!" Hedy called, giving us a start. "Don't those doughnuts have egg in them?" She eyed our treat, setting two plastic bags on the table and pulling out a chair. Then she tossed her head back, fluffed her hair, and smiled up at the sun. "Oh, that feels good. We're finally done with winter."

Nick watched her, enthralled. Wherever Hedy goes, she moves in a private magnetic field, and you can almost watch molecules of energy stir about her. Hedy, you see, is a beauty. Tall, with lush raven hair, fine features, and a flair for the dramatic. She has a patrician bearing that comes from her height. She's at least five feet nine, but unlike many tall women she never stoops, she's at ease with her stature and luxuriates in it. I still see the lovely young woman in her, although the turquoise eye shadow she uses – Nick likes it, she once told me – really doesn't suit anybody at sixty. No matter who says it, sixty's not the new forty.

"I've got some gems," she said, one hand gesturing at the bags. Today she'd pinned a silky purple bow behind her right ear, in a girlish touch.

Hedy's question about the doughnuts wasn't related to cholesterol, though we were at that time of life when people talk about high blood pressure and the like. After they'd married, she and Nick discovered an Indian guru with a teaching called The Way. They called it the sum of all religions: worldly attachment caused suffering. Those culprits, the senses, and their pals, the appetites, lie in wait to ambush you. Abstinence was the only escape: no alcohol, tobacco, or drugs; married couples were even urged to refrain from sexual relations as much as possible. The goal was to be done with the cycle of reincarnation. An egg was a potential life, a part of the cycle, and eating one tied you to trouble.

Hedy and I had met in the ninth grade. Back then she ate cheeseburgers like everyone else, but she also attended hush-hush meetings at the local library, where the neighborhood Rosicrucians talked about whatever they talked about. (Strange, how you never hear of Rosicrucians anymore.) As long as I've known Hedy, she's been drawn to secret learning and arcane wisdom.

"Want a tea, hon?" Nick asked.

"I just need to rest a minute, before we go to the mall. This sun's glorious."

The mall she spoke of was the Oberlin Antique Mall, several miles outside the city.

"You're sure you're coming?" she asked me. "I'll be at our booth for a couple hours."

Hedy checked newspaper and internet ads for estate sales, and with an eye for the rare find, often came up with some neglected treasure which she sold at the mall or on eBay. She was also a gifted potter, and her small sculpture animals had a following across the state, where they were in the collections of several museums. But the onset of arthritis now slowed her down.

"Every day," she said, "it gets harder. And I feel like we're losing more freedom."

Nick nodded gravely. "Surely you can feel it happening? It's chaos out there."

"Nick's upset about things," Hedy said. "We feel like this isn't our country anymore."

"That's it exactly," he agreed. "My country's been taken away from me."

"I don't see chaos. The cars aren't on the sidewalk…" I stopped. When our visits took this turn, I flipped into irony. But it's a confining refuge, especially if you can't share it.

They looked at each other conspiratorially, then back at me.

Nick and Hedy insisted that the President's birth certificate was forged – they'd seen the proof on line – and that he was out to destroy the country. Greedy unions and liberal professors and illegal Hispanics and ridiculous regulations were also doing their part. It was too easy to call this nonsense. Anyway, I consider most politicians opportunists. That's not the point, though. My facts weren't theirs, my sources made them sneer. If I cited the

New York Times, they countered with Rush Limbaugh. Conservatives loved America and progressives hated it. Period.

The sun was bright but the day had darkened. I could try to change the subject and tell them about the theft in the library. Or ask Nick what he was working on.

Nick had gone to graduate school in literature, but never completed his doctoral thesis. Instead, he wrote poetry, though he has yet to publish a collection. When Guy came along, Nick took a job in an uncle's car dealership, inheriting it after a decade. He ran the business for a few years and had a nervous collapse, but did well selling it. Since then he and Hedy have lived off its legacy, along with the top up from her discoveries, which Nick packed for mailing.

We hadn't met for several weeks and I was anxious about the afternoon, when they were coming to lunch at my place. "I made mushroom stroganoff," I said. A favorite of theirs.

Hedy took my cue. "Here, let me show you this." She pulled a small parcel from one of the bags and began to unwrap it. On each wrist she wore a thick copper bracelet meant to cut the pain from arthritis and rebalance her chakras, or something like that. The newspaper wrapping fell back to reveal a cobalt blue glass tumbler. Depression ware, the kind once given away on movie-theater prize nights. "Perfect condition," Hedy observed. On one side of the tumbler was a silvery white decal of curly-haired Shirley Temple, a smiling, ghostly image.

"I paid only a quarter, and it's worth thirty dollars at least."

"Ask forty," Nick said. This wasn't one of her better finds, but they were pleased with it.

During our ride to the mall, I tried to keep the talk on congenial subjects, though even the weather wasn't a safe one because Nick and Hedy considered global warming a scientific hoax. Several miles out of town, we parked by a warehouse-like building. Over fifty thousand square feet, the mall held more than two hundred booths in long wide rows. Everything from rare china figurines to Bakelite jewelry, turn-of-the-last-century pottery to fur coats from the forties, art-deco lamps and Victorian dog engravings, even fragile Christmas ornaments, gave the place an air of an eccentric grandma's attic. Since the booths are mostly unattended, floorwalkers patrol them, tagging objects for prospective buyers and taking these to the front service desk.

Following Nick, I carried several heavy cardboard boxes to their booth in the third aisle. I wondered if Sheila would be in her booth today, and hoped not.

"Thanks for your help," Hedy said. "I don't want Nick to strain himself. He's been having trouble with his rotator cuff. I worry all the time."

Several years younger than Hedy, Nick stood at least six feet two inches tall, a trim man with the dark, Italianate good looks that still turned heads. His family name was Antonacci, but as a young man Nick had legally shortened it to Anton: that would look better on his first book of poems. Long ago we'd agreed that young men had to invent themselves.

"We have to take care of each other," Nick joined in. "I'm constantly worrying, too. I hate it when she goes out to her estate sales – she's a good driver, it's the others I worry about."

"You know I'm fine," Hedy stopped him, and began unpacking. As if reading my mind, she added, "I don't want him to drive me, I feel hurried then, and I need to take my time."

It can be tricky for anyone single to be close to couples, married or not. "I think I'll look around," I told them, heading off. It usually took me an hour to walk the mall, browsing for first editions. Three aisles to the right I spotted Sheila's booth, but she was nowhere in sight.

I've known Sheila Carney for ten years. She used to have an antiques shop in town, but as the recession cut into business she closed her doors and rented a booth in the mall. She also ran estate sales when she was lucky enough to know the family of someone who'd died, or a lawyer who did. And she worked at odd jobs like gardening. One summer, when the weeds in my yard got out of hand, I'd hired her, and she planted herself there. Since antique dealers attend the same auctions and estate sales, rivalries flare. Hedy had no use for Sheila and called her coarse, while Sheila thought Nick and Hedy pretentious. Each, in a way, was probably right.

Few customers ambled about today, as if a bomb threat had cleared the mall. An antiquarian bookseller named Claire Warren had the booth across from Sheila's, and I stopped there to check out her latest arrivals.

"Are you with your friends?" Sheila called from down the aisle. She must have spotted Nick or Hedy.

"We're having lunch today," I said.

Frowning, Sheila lugged a large cardboard box. "Easter things," she explained. "I'm running late this year. And I need the money. Badly."

Sheila lived pretty much from hand to mouth. At the mall she specialized in antique linens and obscure kitchen utensils, such domestic stuff. At the back of the booth her doll collection, locked away in a glass case, was staring out vacantly.

"Your Lady Hedda," she groaned, shaking her head.

"Please, Sheila…"

She stuck her tongue out, laughed, and set the box on the seat of a pressed-back oak kitchen chair that was marked "$45."

"Did they tell you about Guy?" I said.

"What about him?"

Now she was curious. Guy often spent Saturday afternoons at the mall, manning the family booth, and Sheila was very fond of him. "He's moving out…"

"That's old news," she cut me off. "Never mind, I feel like hell. My hot flashes…"

At fifty, Sheila was struggling with her body. She'd recently dyed her hair the bronze color of a Coppertone bottle, and had it streaked with ox-blood red gashes. "Six bucks a streak!" she'd complained. Of course she worked at maintaining her weight, and still had a good figure.

"I thought you'd heard something about Guy's find," Sheila added.

"What find?"

"Didn't his parents tell you? Last month he bought an old box full of letters at an estate sale. It turns out three of them are from the woman who wrote *Uncle Tom's Cabin*."

"Harriet Beecher Stowe? Have you seen them?"

"No. Guy went to an expert. Some people get all the breaks."

"But you wouldn't have bought old letters."

"Let's not talk about it."

Something more was troubling her. "Have you heard from Brad again?"

"Don't ask. Don't go there. I mean it. Really."

Brad was the boyfriend. A house painter when he worked. Ten years younger than Sheila, he drank his pay as fast as he earned it. "I'm crazy about him," she'd often told me while pruning something or other. "I'm crazy in love."

"Why do you bother with those people?" she said, changing the subject.

"We go back a long time, Hedy and me. Practically forever."

"Well, they've ruined their kid," she objected. "He's afraid of his shadow. But I've got a great pair of bronze bookends for him," she added. "For housewarming."

Guy collected books about the Civil War, and military memorabilia related to it. It made no sense, this meek boy interested in veterans' medals and old daggers. Hedy said that he'd seen *Gone With the Wind* in the sixth grade and had been

13

bowled over. Nick explained that the market for military collectibles was stable and lucrative, which Guy understood.

"I should think of something for him, too. I'll ask Nick what he needs."

"Look, I'd better get down to work. Do you want me to start cleaning up the garden tomorrow morning?"

Spring cleanup is a serious matter in our part of the state, a snow belt. We didn't mention Brad again. If he appeared tonight, my yard would have to wait.

Curious about Guy's letters, I headed back to the Antons' booth. Most of the mall's visitors are over fifty, and with money tight, only the savviest dealers can keep afloat. Television programs like *Antiques Roadshow* have made people aware of the value in family heirlooms, even in cast-off junk. That Shirley Temple tumbler might be a holy grail to someone reassembling a childhood from other people's discards.

"We were about to send out the scouts," Nick said as I approached.

"He was with Sheila," Hedy remarked. "I told you that."

"We have to get back to Guy," Nick said. "I promised to help him pack some things later, and we need to hit the road right after lunch if we're going to meditate first."

Regular meditation, I should add, was part of their beliefs.

"What did Sheila have to say?" Hedy asked, reaching for her purse. She took out a mirror and a tube of red lipstick, quickly painted her mouth, pressed her lips together, checked her face in the mirror, and then looked up at me. "She must have said something."

"Nothing special."

"Really? But she's so full of herself."

"That's for sure," Nick added.

I almost said, "Aren't we all?"

2

The theft at the library's archives preoccupied me all the next week, and I'd barely noticed that the heat wave had sputtered out. When I turned into my driveway after work, anticipating a double Scotch, I found Sheila digging at the edges of my front-yard flower bed. Though I never intended this, my garden has become the best on the block, a romantic English money-pit.

"I thought I'd check a few things," she called. Of course she really wanted to talk, her eyes said as much. As she followed me into the house I said, "You seem frazzled. What's up?"

"I can't afford to lose another client. It's tough when friends move away."

Friends and clients were a heady mix for Sheila – a confusion she fostered. I'd guessed this when she first arrived to solve my gardening problems with a batch of homemade brownies.

"Who's moving?"

"Theo Eliades. To Bay Village. He told me yesterday, when I phoned about cleaning up his garden."

"But you knew his house was for sale. He'll be closer to Daphne."

Theo hadn't called me yet. We were friends from campus, for over a decade, where he'd worked in the counseling office. Worn down by being understanding and supportive, he'd taken early retirement. Fraternal twins, he and Daphne often spoke of their childhood, both claiming to have clairvoyant powers, special instincts, intuitions.

I had no idea what Sheila wanted Theo to do. Her attitude was typical of many outside the academic community in a small college town. While our common resembles a page from an idyllic New England calendar, tensions have existed between the farming community and the college since it was plopped down in the middle of a cornfield in 1833. From its start, the college has been progressive: the first in the U.S. to be co-ed; the first to welcome black students, in 1835; then, a stop on the Underground Railway. Today the town and gown split still divides us.

Like everyone on campus, I was glad to see February finished. Swastikas had been spray-painted on posters for Black History month, and signs for "Whites Only" taped over several drinking fountains. Then one Sunday night a student driving past the Center for Women and Transgender People spotted somebody in a white robe and hood. The next day classes were cancelled for a solidarity rally. As anger grew, a police official suggested that the Klan sighting might be a hoax. But who else wore such hoods? Of course security alerts filled each day, the national media showed up, and CNN anchors put the spotlight on us. Anyhow, I wasn't in the mood for Sheila's complaints, though she has a good bullshit detector.

"Well, it's like everybody's moving," she repeated. "But why Bay Village? Do they want to be murdered?"

"Her place is by the lake." I lit a fire under the kettle for tea. An affluent suburb west of Cleveland, Bay Village is still known for a sixty-year-old crime, when the osteopath Sam Sheppard killed his pregnant wife, Marilyn, but claimed that a bushy-haired intruder was guilty. The case later inspired a popular television series and movie. "Are you going to tell me what's bothering you?"

"Brad's seeing someone else."

"You've known that for months, Sheila."

"Yeah, but she's out to drive me crazy. She keeps phoning in the middle of the night and hanging up as soon as I answer. The number's blocked so I can't do a thing about it."

"You could turn off your ringer."

"But it might be my mother. You know she had a mastectomy last year."

"Fair enough." Just fifty, Sheila still had a living parent; your life feels different then.

"Mind if I smoke? I'm down to five a day and I need one now."

I handed her an ashtray from under the sink. "How do you know it's Brad's girlfriend? And does she have a name?"

"Loretta." Sheila searched her purse for her smokes. "She's thirty-five. Younger than Brad. And in and out of the county jail, half a dozen times. If only I didn't love him so much."

"What was she in for?"

"Drugs, shoplifting. I think she also turns tricks." Sheila took a drag of her cigarette, choked, and mumbled, "Shit. You know, I'm still head over heels. It's been five years next month. Five years down the drain. That's a long time."

The kettle whistled and I reached to pour hot water over tea bags.

"Hey, don't bother with any for me. Brad says it's not Loretta. And unless he's lying, they aren't sleeping together anymore. Maybe he wants to get back with me. Oh, the hell with it." Shrugging, she paused. "You know, I saw Guy's new place. It's tough, starting over like this."

"He's hardly starting over, he's growing up."

"Blame that on your friends." She stubbed her cigarette.

"Can we leave them out of this?" We were talking in circles. I wanted to cook my supper, drink my Scotch, and take a hot shower.

"He's seeing a therapist. Just don't tell them. Guy says they'd disown him."

"For seeing a therapist? I doubt it, Sheila. His parents are devoted."

"Screw devotion," she said. "I should be moving on – there's always too much to do."

"The garden looks great, Sheila. It needed your touch."

"I know," she agreed. And then she was gone.

The evening would be shot if I didn't watch out. With Sheila's funk lingering, I decided to phone Theo. His house had sold in a terrible market.

"Hullo," he said, almost too softly to hear, as if he'd been polishing his depression like the family silver. No anti-pills, Theo didn't go in for those, just sitting immobile.

"Sheila said you've got good news. We should celebrate."

"I don't think I could do that. Not today. It's so final now."

"But this is what you wanted. Are you worrying about Neil? He'll be fine."

For the last year, Theo had rented the spare room in his house to Neil Breuler, who worked as a campus security guard and had once helped him change a flat tire on his Volvo. Turning fifty, Neil had just left his wife of twenty years. Perhaps Theo loved him. There was nothing sexual between them, Theo told me so, yet Neil appeared to plump up on his attention, his fussing, and Theo couldn't help himself.

"Have you been checking out Neil's room again?"

Once, Theo had mentioned that he'd done some snooping, almost courting an objection.

"Well," he stammered. "I've given it another look-see. I have to know what's going on in my own house, don't I? Wouldn't you do the same thing?"

"Frankly, I can't imagine renting out my spare room. What did you find?"

"Just his stuff. I didn't look that carefully. But nothing out of the ordinary."

"C'mon, Theo, you're holding back…"

"He has several boxes of condoms. Some were even flavored. Banana and chocolate."

"Just ordinary stuff," I repeated. "Okay. Do you have any supper plans?"

He didn't answer at once.

"Then come on, let's have a pizza."

"I could ask Neil to join us."

"No, Theo, just you and me and the pizza. Neil can fend for himself. He's a big boy."

"Maybe another night? I don't really feel like company. We'll talk later."

Two depressives in one afternoon – my limit. What, I had to ask, was friendship about? A troubled friendship's like drowning, you can't breathe, but when you stop seeing an old friend you lose a part of yourself. Naturally my thoughts returned to Hedy and Nick. We were no longer allies, a childish notion perhaps but friendship's shadow.

During our lunch at my place we'd reminisced about old times, until I brought up Guy's discovery.

"Who told you?" Hedy asked.

"Sheila did. Is it a secret?"

Nick leaned towards me. "Sheila knew?"

"Guy told her. Of course I'm curious. The archive has a good collection of documents related to Oberlin during the Civil War."

"We don't want to broadcast it," cautioned Hedy. "You know, people would like to get hold of the letters and take credit for finding them."

"I wonder who Stowe was writing to," I said, ignoring the rest.

"We did a little research," Hedy replied in a softer tone. "In the 1840s she was living in Cincinnati with her father, a Presbyterian minister, and they might have visited the college."

I wanted to hear more. "What were the letters like?"

"We haven't seen them," Nick explained. "Guy took them to an expert right away."

"But what makes him think they're from Stowe? Was her name on an envelope?"

"Guy said the writer mentions a novel she was completing," added Hedy, almost protectively. "And she signed her first name *Harriet*."

Skepticism was probably the wrong tack. "I hope Guy gets good advice."

"He will," Hedy assured me, shifting about uncomfortably in her chair.

"Are your knees acting up?" I asked.

"They've been worse," she said with a shrug. "Today I want to forget I have knees."

Years ago the Antons had looked forward to a retirement of travel abroad, and we'd mentioned trips together, to Tuscany, maybe Venice; all happy dreams. But Hedy's arthritis now made even local treks difficult.

"We've been really worried about what's going on in the country," Nick said, as if his thoughts had piled up on him and he had to speak out or suffocate. "We're losing faith in it."

I didn't ask why. With the presidential primaries in full swing, could we avoid them?

Naturally Hedy chimed in. "All the talk of same-sex marriage in California and Washington…"

"How can that matter to you?" I took the bait. "It's not important to me, I can't imagine wanting to get married. And no matter who gets married, it doesn't touch you and Nick."

"Yes, it does. It devalues us. What we've made together."

"Marriage has always meant a man and a woman," Nick agreed. "And the children."

"Well, that's changing. We're talking about civil rights, legal…"

"Civilizations have ended over less," Hedy warned. "Remember that."

"What are you talking about?" I asked.

"You don't think we're the only civilization that's lived on the planet?" Her mouth tightened into a nervous smile. "Ice ages have wiped out others, but they existed."

The ice age and same-sex marriage – too big a leap for me.

"I probably don't like change any more than you do, but it isn't always for the worse," I said, not wanting to placate her. "Anyway, you can't stop time…"

"We're not bigots," Nick interrupted me.

"It started with the military." Hedy shook her head. "I wouldn't want to be a young soldier and have to shower with lesbians looking at my body. We owe our soldiers more."

"But gays are serving in armies all around the world without a catastrophe. In Israel…"

"This has got nothing to do with you," Nick stopped me. "You know we care about you. And you know we're not bigots."

Apparently there was to be no disagreement between us about that. Did they assume I bedded down with a new body every night? I couldn't guess what they thought.

Nick reached across the table and folded his hand over mine. As I started to pull away, he pressed his hand against my wrist and held it there, to the table. "If two men or women love each other, we wish them well, but that's not the point."

"Sure it is. That's exactly the point. You'd better be careful about the kind of the people who share your views."

"Don't you believe in liberty?" Nick stared at me as if I'd somehow lost my bearings.

"Liberty's not the point. We can have different values, but facts are facts," I said. "We can't have different facts."

Hedy frowned, about to reply, as Nick continued: "A lot of people think like us. Don't underestimate that."

"It's true." She nodded approvingly.

I glanced down at the table, at Nick's hand on mine. When they spoke like this I'd come to feel it didn't matter if I was in the room with them, they were only talking to themselves. They both knew that I'd been part of the Vietnam War exodus of young men to Canada, when the powers that be used my generation as cannon fodder. Though I now lived back in the U.S., I carried two passports – you can never have too many passports.

It's 2012, I told myself, not the 1950s. Joe McCarthy wasn't running amok, no campus required a loyalty oath. And yet, what would the world be like if the Tea Party had its way? Watching Hedy, I tried to remember the young girl I'd met half a century ago, the girl who sat across from me in art class and noticed my fumbles with a charcoal pencil. She'd leaned over the table and said, "Hold it like this, at an angle," demonstrating patiently.

After class we'd walked to the cafeteria together. She strode along like she owned the corridors of our high school, and I loved her ease. Hedy had no interest in its cliques or home games. Back when everyone listened to the Beatles and folk music, we preferred Beethoven, dreamed of visiting Europe's museums, impatient to graduate. She was studying the cello for a concert career. I can still see her giving a solo recital, one of Bach's unaccompanied sonatas, in the small auditorium of the local library where I worked as a page. She'd borrowed her mother's French perfume and its scent somehow drew attention away from the music. I understood, then, that our bond had been sealed because I wasn't looking for a girlfriend, and never would.

"You know us as well as anybody," Nick said. "We have principled beliefs."

The weight of his hand on my wrist began to anger me. "I guess we'll have to agree to disagree," I said, drawing my hand back. Before me sat an old married couple united by love – it was hard to tell where one ended and the other began.

After high-school graduation, Hedy had spent a few years at Juilliard, but she suffered an injury to her shoulder, couldn't practice long hours, and went home to recover. By then I'd left the country and, in that world before e-mail, we kept in touch with just birthday cards and holiday greetings. Almost twenty years later I returned to Oberlin for a job at the college, and we resumed our friendship as if we were the same people. That first winter my father died, dementia began to claim my mother, and she had to move in with me. Then her decline sped up, and Hedy and Nick often visited us, always including her in our talks, never showing impatience. I still felt grateful to them for that. But I was perplexed. What had hardened such caring friends, making them angry and fearful? They were good people; *are* good people.

"If we were younger," Hedy said, "I'd want Nick to run for office. He'd be great, he's so sensitive. But the system's rigged." She watched her husband's broadening smile. "Well, that's what I think. Don't be embarrassed, dear."

I was always glad they didn't bicker in front of me the way couples sometimes do, as if it's a rite of married love. And yet it seemed wise to change the subject – I did a lot of that – and ask Hedy about any new sculptures.

"I have some photographs on my cell phone," Nick said, reaching for it.

"Don't show him," Hedy said, her face tightening in a grimace. I drew back as if slapped.

"Oh, no, I want to, hon," Nick said, fiddling with his phone and ignoring her.

"He won't like them," Hedy insisted.

"What do you mean? I've always liked your work."

"They're not really your style." Her face clouded with an unidentifiable emotion.

Hyper real, her ceramic creatures stood as proof of the time she'd spent studying sculpting, glazing, firing. Perhaps Hedy was miffed that I hadn't bought something at her exhibition last fall, but I already owned one five-hundred-dollar raccoon.

Nick held up some images and I said they were full of life.

"Of course he liked them," Nick said.

He, him, he…

Hedy stared out the dining-room window, at branches of forsythia in yellow profusion. What kind of test had I nearly failed? Still, we made plans for a day of antiquing, yet I'd felt only saddened when they left.

Frustrated by the memory, I crossed my study, searched its bookshelves, and found a worn paperback from my undergraduate days: Aristotle's *Nicomachean Ethics*, with his thoughts about friendship. I needed some help. The words *exchange* and *goodness* came back to mind. Friendship has to have an ethical dimension – this I did remember. After the last week, I'd had my fill of friends so I unplugged the telephone. With a Scotch finally in hand, I cracked open the book.

An hour later, the doorbell interrupted my reading. Though the house had darkened, I didn't turn on another lamp. Even rooms known well can seem ominous in the dark. Once all the lights are on, will they be the same as you left them? When I opened the front door, Theo Eliades stood there, looking sheepish. "Your answering machine's off and I started to worry."

"I didn't mean to worry you, Theo. Sorry, I'm fine. Come on in. Want a drink?"

"I'd like to but Neil's waiting for me. We're going for some Chinese chow, you could join us. He's treating me tonight. I just wanted to make sure you were still alive."

We both laughed. Until then I hadn't noticed Theo's car parked at the curb with Neil in the driver's seat. I couldn't hear if the motor was running.

"Well, I am. Alive as I can be."

3

Two of Hedy's raccoons were posed to scamper across the fire-place mantel, while at the opposite end an unfamiliar creature peered at them.

"Is that a skunk?" I asked. I didn't think Hedy made skunks. "No, wait, it looks like a badger."

"That's right," Guy said, grinning, with the whitest teeth I'd ever seen.

"Badgers in this part of the country?"

"It's from an old British book," Guy said. "I found it for Mom at an estate sale."

The badger's head appeared to be turned upwards and cocked to the left, as if a sound had startled it during a nocturnal hunt or while guarding its cubs. Amazing that a clay creature could seem frozen in time like this.

"When I was seven she read me *The Wind in the Willows*, and after that I always wanted a pet badger." He paused for a moment, perhaps lost in a memory. "Here, I'll show you around. I'm still unpacking."

I wasn't exactly sure why I'd come to see Guy. Maybe Sheila's talk made me ashamed that I hadn't bothered to know him better.

In any small town, even a few blocks can make a big demographic difference. Guy's place was located in Oberlin's southeast corner, not far from the Groveland and Pleasant Street intersection, the center of our roughest neighborhood. That is, if you can use the word *rough* for something this ordinary. While marijuana is popular with students, hard drugs predominate here. There's not much local crime, mainly breaking and entering and petty thefts, but most of it originates nearby. Sheila lived a short walk away, but on a better block.

The 1920s bungalow sported a few arts-and-crafts features, like beveled glass windows, and an American flag the size of a large dinner napkin had been attached to the post of the porch's wood railing. The living room where we stood was empty except for a black leather recliner, a pole lamp behind it, and a new flat-screen television on an oak stand. No newspapers or magazines in sight.

"I'm not in a hurry to buy things," Guy said, and I followed him into the dining room, where only a large oak bookcase stood against one wall. Three shelves held his collection of Civil War memorabilia, and history books filled the rest. I glanced quickly at a canteen, a belt buckle, a box of cartridges, what appeared to be a regimental cup, and several rows of medals and badges.

"You've got quite a collection."

He smiled modestly. "Just the beginning."

Half a dozen small frames contained bleary photographs of long-dead young soldiers. Like his parents, Guy probably believed in reincarnation, and perhaps thought he'd been at Gettysburg or Antietam.

"Here's the kitchen," he said, moving away from the bookcase. Over the years we'd spent very little time together, and he must have felt awkward. "I like painting. After a while it reminds me of meditation, when you get into it."

"You've done a good job."

"I hope so." He looked around as if uncertain that the room belonged to him. "Sheila did the cupboards, it was real nice of her. Mom says you know her, too."

"She's looked after my garden for ages."

"I'll bet she's good at that. My landlady says I can do whatever I want with the yard. She said I could even plant potatoes, she doesn't care, as long as I mow the lawn. Sheila's going to show me what's growing out there."

A 1950s dinette set with a red Formica-topped table was pushed against one wall. Over it hung a framed movie poster from *Gone With the Wind*, though probably not an original.

"I brought you something," I said, handing him a shopping bag that contained a largish cardboard box. "For a housewarming."

"A present!" He grinned again, but sheepishly, and took the electric kettle from its box. "This is great, thanks. It's a really good make."

"If you already have one…"

"I don't. This is great." Then he laughed and said, "You can't have it back."

"No, no. It's yours forever." I was beginning to see why Sheila liked him.

Guy set the kettle on the counter and looked as if he were going to pat it. Only then did I notice a small framed photograph of a handsome, dark-skinned man with a snow-white turban and genial smile. The guru, of course; I'd seen a similar picture at the Antons.

Tall, like his father, and with his mother's fine features and raven hair, though closely cropped to a Velcro fuzz, Guy might have been twenty-four, not ten years older. Without trying, I could see the impress of a young girl named Hedy on his face, the same strong brow, high cheek bones, and aquiline nose. The same heart shape and bow lips.

"Would you like a Coke? I'm out of tea, I haven't been grocery shopping."

An alcohol-free zone, like Hedy and Nick's?

"Sure," I said, and pulled a kitchen chair out from the table as he went to the refrigerator. There was nothing on the table but an empty wooden napkin holder and Guy's cell phone.

He wore a loose gray T-shirt and old jeans, torn at the knees – the uniform du jour – and his lanky long arms had an orangey glow, as if he'd done time in a tanning booth.

"What made you settle here?" I asked.

"It's close to my new job. At the clinic." He set the cans of soda on the table. "I don't have any nibbles," he apologized. "I'm trying to eat healthy, you know. Want a glass?"

"No, thanks, this is fine. So you like your work? What does a dental technician do?" I snapped the tab on my drink.

"Dental hygienist," he corrected. "A little of everything. Cleaning, checking gums, polishing, fluoride treatments. Even whitening."

That explained his bright smile. "There's not much left for the dentist."

"They do the fillings and extractions. It's a pretty good job. I can bike to work and meet interesting people from the college, you'd be surprised. And it doesn't take up mental space, there's still time to think about my eBay sales, important things. Like this summer, Mom and Dad and I are driving down to Columbus, to the APIC convention."

"The what?"

"American Political Items Collectors. We've got some great old presidential campaign buttons. Really mint Eisenhower buttons. And Goldwater, too."

What fed into such nostalgia?

Guy looked at me intently. "You know, total sales for the convention could reach five million."

"That's hard to believe, but the rare book market often surprises me. I'm sure your parents appreciate your help."

Sheila had told me Guy was eager to move out on his own, and here I was, asserting his family's claims. Would he like living alone? Hedy or Nick might give me updates. I wondered what Guy thought of the shift in their politics, or if he ever asked for their sources and argued about them. Maybe he bought into their views, a Tea Party junior. Those Goldwater buttons made me pause.

"I've started to set up an office in the basement," he confided. "I'll show you, if you like. Soon I can use the spare bedroom for working out and meditating."

His cell phone beeped, Guy looked down at it, squinted, and said, "I'll get that later."

"I don't want to keep you from unpacking."

"Oh, no, don't think that. Please."

"We've never talked by ourselves, Guy, your parents were always there. Everything I know about you comes from them."

"That's alright," he said calmly.

Perhaps I'd been wrong to mention it. "You'll like Oberlin," I said, to fill a gap of silence. I sounded like a retired volunteer for the Chamber of Commerce.

"I already do. Big cities aren't for me. Too much crime. Now I can easily check on our booth at the mall, Mom and Dad won't have to bother so often, and I can help Sheila, too. She shouldn't be lugging heavy things."

Was he always this selfless? The idea of Sheila painting anyone's cupboards had caught my attention. Perhaps she was keen on Guy, she did prefer younger men.

"If you need anything, you know you can call on me. It's not easy being new in town."

He flashed one of his enthusiastic wide smiles. Puppyish.

"I heard about your letters from Harriet Beecher Stowe, they're quite a find. You'll be famous. What made you buy the box? Something drew you to it."

"I never thought anything like that would happen to me. Really. It was nice wood, and I like reading old letters. It's kind of like time travel, or an episode of *History Detectives*, if you know what I mean."

"I think so. It's part of archival work. I'd be glad to look at them sometime." I hoped he didn't think I came by only because of the letters.

"Right now they're with a paper expert in Buffalo. At the university's Center for Document Analysis. I drove them there myself, I didn't want to trust FedEx."

Guy seemed happy to talk about the letters and I wondered why Hedy had hesitated to mention them. Since our last visit I'd read up on Stowe. At twenty-one she moved from Connecticut to Cincinnati, to teach school. Her first encounters with slavery took place there and she became a convert to the abolitionist movement. The chapters that made up *Uncle Tom's Cabin* appeared as a serial in an anti-slavery newspaper, were published as a book in 1852, and soon became an international sensation.

"If you can authenticate your letters..." I began to say.

"Then they'll probably go to Sotheby's for auction. That's what I'd like."

"The college archive might be interested, especially with any connection to Oberlin. I could put up a small exhibition at the library, people would be fascinated."

"I'll remember, I promise. I'm gonna put up my own website for Civil War memorabilia, there's a good market for it. You should check out the internet."

"How did you get so interested in the Civil War?"

He looked surprised by my question. "I always was," he said.

"Maybe your time in the army had something to do with it – a sympathy for soldiers?"

"I don't know." He laughed then, with an easy, self-deprecating tone. "You see, every summer, from my tenth birthday on, Mom and Dad left me with my grandparents in Knoxville for a month. We used to drive through the Appalachians and to different battle sites. I loved it and started collecting stuff. First, postcards, then old Confederate money."

"That must have been before I got my job here," I said, not wanting to sound like a cross-examination.

"Guess so. I really liked Knoxville. Do you know it?"

I shook my head. Five summers ago I had my last fling, with a sweet, unhappily divorced colleague who, late in August, took a better position at the university there. Relieved, I'd wished him well. That fall he sent several postcards of the Smokeys, a letter about his children's new school, and then vanished for good. Guy didn't need to hear any of this.

"Grandma's dead now so I haven't been back since, but I'd like to live there. She died when I was fourteen."

"Yet you chose Oberlin."

"Maybe someday I'll move south," he mused, ignoring my remark. "But I'm gonna like it here. C'mon, I'll show you the rest of the place."

I was glad to see him smiling, and light-hearted. As we stood up, his cell phone rang again. "I'll get it later," he said, without looking at the caller's number.

"You're already popular," I teased.

"I wouldn't like that."

4

When I got around to googling "Civil War memorabilia," as Guy had suggested, it amazed me to find numerous on-line dealers with large war-time collections. You could even buy a complete Confederate lieutenant's uniform for a hundred grand. The dealers were scattered across the country, with many in New England, though most of them specialized in Southern souvenirs, and even used that old term, the War of Northern Aggression. But what surprised me most were the pop-ups that kept appearing from site to site. "Eye on Muslim Threat" one proclaimed, "Pro-Israeli Posters" beckoned another. Several advertised "Obama Fake Birth Certificate!" Was the phrase "Civil War memorabilia" a code for paramilitary sympathies or Tea Party outrage? Apparently Guy was Nick and Hedy's intellectual heir, a true believer, while the path to enlightenment welcomed battle cries. Ignoring the pop-ups, I'd learned enough. I felt uneasy, disquieted, although no one could have guessed what was about to happen.

During several days of persistent rain I tried to forget my last visit with Hedy and Nick. One gray afternoon I headed over to Claire Warren's booth at the mall. She'd sent several e-mails about new acquisitions, so I thought I'd take a look. The aisles appeared abandoned, but two clerks, marooned behind the check-out station, chatted amiably.

"Hey, stranger," Claire greeted me.

Unlike the stereotype of an antiquarian bookseller as tweedy and withdrawn, Claire had long ago decided to be bigger than life. With family money behind her she didn't need a booth at the mall for income, just distraction. Claire had married and divorced two local professors by her recent "golden jubilee," as she called turning fifty, and now swore off men. Generous to a fault, she was popular with a younger set of academics because of her lavish parties. Her June bashes were much anticipated – she always filled a small plastic wading pool with a martini mix and told her guests to dip their glasses into it for refills. I'd stopped going years ago but she forgave me. And yes, she had a great eye for rare books.

"Have you seen Guy's letters?" she asked at once. "Just watch, he'll make the *New York Times*. Such luck! I hope he knows it."

"But you've been pretty lucky yourself."

"You can't have too much luck," she said. "Trust me on that. He's a bit of a loser, no?"

Taken aback, I said, "In the end we're all losers."

"Oh, you understand me. He's really one-upped his parents, though, they've never had a find like this. And think of all the junior professors hot for such a discovery while Guy just trips over it. What I'd like to know is where the letters came from. Why were they left in a box in someone's attic? I thought I knew every attic in the county."

"I don't have the answer."

"But you'll find out," she said. "We're on the same page. I could do well with those letters. A couple of buyers already come in mind."

"I hope the college is one of them. Talk to Guy."

"Did you know that van Gogh loved *Uncle Tom's Cabin*? One of his portraits shows a woman reading the novel, the title's right there on the book."

"Tell that to Guy, too."

"Now real luck would be coming across an unknown van Gogh sketch. I'd even settle for a good forgery. I suppose you think that's wicked. "

"Is that what you'd like? To be wicked?"

"Forgery is all the rage."

You had to laugh along with Claire. She wanted her life to be like one of those screwball comedies from the thirties, where Katharine Hepburn flounced about, but poor Claire, she was stuck without a good script or a good director. There was nothing special in the books she had to show me. She probably knew this but needed an excuse to keep in touch. Or to pump me about Guy.

That night, on my way home from campus, I decided to stop at Gibson's, to buy some doughnuts for breakfast and the local paper. I'd worked late and twilight had started to darken the sky, along with ominous rain clouds.

As I hurried along West Lorain, I thought to cut across the common by the Memorial Arch, a neo-classical tribute to the town's missionaries killed somewhere in China back in 1900. Carved into capital letters over one side, the word *MASSACRED* cries out for revenge. This paean to evangelical zeal had been put up three years later, and generations of students have passed blithely by. On graduation day parents like to stand their sons and daughters against the graceful stone curves for a photo op, ignoring the long-forgotten dead.

While crossing Professor Street I spotted two men near the archway. They appeared to be arguing although I couldn't quite make out their words. Hard to say why, but something about them suggested tension or bad feelings. One of them, with his back to me, leaned against his bicycle, seemed propped up by it, while the other, wearing a red windbreaker, was bent towards him, their heads bowed, their faces close together, intimate yet estranged. "But I told you…" or words to that effect came to me in a gust of wind. For an instant I thought I recognized the man in the red windbreaker, his mouth moving emphatically. I paused, rethinking my path across the common in order to avoid them, but it was too late, he'd already seen me, he'd straightened up, stood tall, so I kept walking forward.

"Hello, Neil," I said, about to hurry past him until the second man turned to face me.

It was Guy holding onto the bike. For a moment he stared at me blankly.

I thought he'd been crying, which made no sense. "You okay?" I asked.

"How are ya?" Neil Breuler asked. "Long time no see."

"Yes," I agreed. "I haven't been to Theo's in a while."

"We were talking about you just the other night."

"I should give him a call. I'll do that later. How are you, Guy?"

"I'm okay. It's a bad year for allergies," he said, as if some explanation was necessary. "I'm done in by them."

"Tell me about it," Neil said. He must have finished working for the day because he wasn't wearing his security guard's jacket.

"Everyone's saying that," I added. "The pollen count's off the charts."

So we stood there talking about the weather as it began to drizzle, with little protection from the trees overhead.

"I should move to Miami," Neil said.

Guy wiped his hair with his free hand. I couldn't get a read of his expression. Until the night I dropped off the kettle I'd never seen him with anyone but his parents. Something was wrong, but I didn't know him well enough to guess what it might be.

"I went there once," I chimed in. "And they had a hurricane."

"Fuck it," Neil said. "You can't win."

I wanted to say something reassuring to Guy, who was looking past me, anxiously.

"I'd better get going before it really rains. If you need anything, Guy, just call me, okay?"

"I will," he said with half a smile, shifting his weight from one foot to the other.

I nearly mentioned Claire Warren's interest in his Beecher Stowe letters, but for no special reason thought the better of it. "Don't forget," I added. "And get out of this rain."

Both men laughed softly as I hurried ahead, not waving or looking back. By the time I reached my house, the rain had turned into a downpour. With a Glenfiddich in hand, and a Stouffer's mac and cheese in the oven, I thought of phoning Theo. But on nights like this it's best to sit in my living room and listen to the rain hitting the windows, an oddly comforting sound. Of course my mind wandered to Guy and Neil. They seemed unlikely acquaintances. Perhaps Theo would know something; he liked to keep tabs on his friends. He knew the ins and outs of every celebrity breakup, the worst suspicions going. "It's terrible," he'd say, and then launch into the story. Anyhow, I didn't phone Theo.

Instead, I drank my Scotch, ate my macaroni, and went to bed early. From my pillow I could still hear the falling rain. The telephone rang several times with only hang-ups. What a luxury, monitoring the answering machine. I wished my parents were alive, I would like to have talked to them, but no one could phone from the grave. Once the people you care most about are dead, it can be like filling time with the rest.

The thought of Guy nagged at me. His spirits had seemed brighter during my recent visit, but I couldn't be sure of that.

What had Nick and Hedy been like as parents? Certainly they doted on him, of course sharing their convictions. As a family they'd even meditated together, to secure Guy's astral pathway. While he wasn't spoiled, Hedy once said, "Guy's not in a hurry to find himself." This, from someone who started planning her Carnegie Hall debut at fifteen. Now that my friends' distress spilled over their politics like a heavy oil slick, I didn't ask them which side Guy took in the culture wars. Wasn't he the good son?

I looked at Aristotle on my bedside table. It's funny, the associations we make. If I write "Aristotle," a dry philosophy course comes to mind, but "Ari" probably brings up that trophy bride, Jackie Kennedy. Anyway, the earlier Ari was concerned with what can go wrong between friends. Of course he wrote during a non-egalitarian time, and could think about people with words like *superior* or *inferior*. When friendships sour, a confusion between *inferior* and *superior* is often at fault – the superior person feeling unvalued as superior and the inferior chap wanting greater recognition. Applying this idea to my friends, it was clear that they saw themselves as having a superior understanding of just about everything, and they disliked my refusal to acknowledge it. On the other hand, I naturally considered their positions inferior to mine, which they must have sensed. Ari had diagnosed the problem.

The phone rang again, twice: more hang-ups. I didn't want to read now. If a smart guy like Aristotle couldn't find a solution for me, how could I? I might as well fall asleep to the rain.

5

It was Sunday afternoon when the call came, right after lunch. I'd spent the morning with the *New York Times* and too many mugs of coffee. Cautioning myself to stop wasting the day, I turned on the kitchen radio and went to the sink for some washing up. Roberta Flack crooned away to the slick beat of "Killing Me Softly" on a golden oldies program, and for a few minutes my mind went back more decades than I wanted to count, to another spring, another self, with vague recollections of love, and lost love.

"If you're there, pick up," Sheila's voice came over the answering machine. "Have you heard?"

Without hesitating, I reached for the kitchen phone. "Have you heard?" she asked again, in the same breath.

What had Brad and Loretta done now? Bombed her garage? "About what, Sheila?"

"Guy Anton."

"What about him?" I wasn't up for a guessing game.

"He's dead."

"What?"

"He's dead. Just what I said. He's dead."

"How do you know that?"

"It was on the noon news. Don't you ever put on your TV? They found his body this morning."

"Who did?"

"The police. Well, not exactly. His landlady went to his house, don't ask me why, and she found his body in the basement. So she called the police."

"You're sure it was Guy?"

Roberta Flack was now starting "Will You Still Love Me Tomorrow" and I turned off the radio.

"Just saw it on TV. It looks like he had a bad fall, the poor kid, they're not saying."

"I wonder if Hedy and Nick…"

"The police would've called them, they have to know. My mother plays bridge with his landlady, I'm gonna call her."

"I'd better phone Hedy," I said.

"You'd better," she agreed. "It's awful, he was just getting his life together. We'll talk later, okay?"

Finishing at the sink, I remembered Guy standing before the old rolltop desk in his basement, proudly pointing out its secret compartments, as if they awaited important state secrets; I could see him at Nick and Hedy's, filling their SUV with boxes for the mall; I even imagined him arranging his Civil War treasures on the shelves of his bookcase, deciding which went where, moving them about. A tall, lean young man who was the picture of good health, a poster boy for clean living. Meditate. Work out. Abstain. Then I recalled our last meeting, really more of an unintended encounter, as he held onto his bicycle while Neil Breuler leaned towards him, almost menacingly. I didn't care for Neil, found him too smooth, too ingratiating. Now the impossible: Guy was dead.

I called Nick's cell-phone number in case he and Hedy were on the road, and she answered after the first ring.

"I've heard," I began. "I'm so sorry."

She didn't reply.

"Hedy? I'm so sorry."

"I'm here."

"Where are you now?

"At home."

"Can I do anything? Can I come over?"

"That would be good," she said softly

"I'll be there in an hour."

"That would be good," she repeated, her voice flat, without expression. Then she added, "Drive carefully."

"Yes, yes."

"We aren't going anywhere." She hung up without a goodbye. They must be in shock. Numb.

I showered and shaved, dressed quickly, and on my way out of town thought to stop at a supermarket to pick up something. A fruit pie would be safe and egg-less, they liked apple pie. Didn't women always take food to the bereaved? Baking at least gave them something to do, a practical gesture. Feeling useless, I grabbed a tin of salted cashews as well, remembering they were a favorite of Nick's. During the drive I kept going over what I might say, but only horrible platitudes came to mind. Their lives had been changed forever, and nothing could be done about it.

Hedy and Nick lived outside Medina in a century-old, white shingle farmhouse set back from the road on half a dozen acres. The cement drive off the highway turned into gravel as it approached their house, and I parked beside a stand of tall fir trees. The old barn had been torn down long ago and a modern garage built in its place, with electricity and water and heat for Hedy's studio at its rear. They'd purchased the property shortly after getting married, though I never understood how they could afford it. Apparently the farmhouse was rundown and needed endless work, but they considered themselves lucky to have found the ideal place back in the 1970s, when the township had yet to become desirable. They even joked that they were pioneers.

It was just shy of four o'clock when I knocked on their front door. The lilacs on either side of it were already open, another sign of early spring. Though it seemed wrong to enjoy their heady lush scent, I took a deep breath as I waited, and then knocked a second time. The house reminded me that my friends were romantics at heart, hoping against hope for creative lives, artists' lives.

Hedy opened the door and, standing back, said, "You're here."

I kissed her right check and fumbled with the grocery bag.

"Come in. You made good time." She grabbed hold of my free arm, steadying herself.

I hadn't seen Hedy without her bright eye shadow and makeup for decades, and the woman standing before me was a paler version of the one I knew. She might have been an older sister, a more tight-lipped version of Hedy. Odd, though, this new woman suited the old farmhouse, with her navy blue pullover almost matching her slacks and none of the dramatic jewelry Hedy usually wore.

"I brought a pie," I offered.

"Nick's resting now. He's devastated. We don't know what to do."

I followed her into the kitchen, put the pie on the counter, and watched as she took it out of the supermarket's plastic bag. "Thank you, this was very thoughtful." As she said the words, almost by rote, they lacked substance.

"It's nothing," I said, struck by her apparent calm. Hedy had always had an iron will, compelling to a restless mind like mine.

"I'll make some tea."

"First, tell me what happened."

"We don't know. They don't know yet."

"Wasn't Guy in good health?"

"Oh, very fit."

I tried to summon his shy half smile and that lost air of a teenage boy.

Hedy's eyes, I saw, were bloodshot.

"He did look fit," I agreed.

"I asked the police if they thought there was a home invasion, something to make Guy go to hide in the basement, but they couldn't say."

We stood in the kitchen as if we'd forgotten it was possible to find chairs and sit comfortably. "I haven't heard of any home invasions in Oberlin," I said.

"They're happening everywhere. The newspapers just don't report them, they don't want to scare us."

I thought the newspapers were quite happy to scare everyone, in fact they thrived on it. "What else did they tell you?"

"His landlady had driven by that morning, Guy was expecting her. She had an extra lawn mower he could use, it would save him money from buying one."

"He was excited about having a yard. He told me that the night I stopped by."

She tried to smile. "When he didn't answer the bell she walked around the house, saw a light on in the basement, and used her own key. That's how she found him."

It was odd, speaking of Guy as if he were dead, and I had to remind myself that he was.

"She called here while we were out. With the police." As soon as Hedy said the word *police*, her eyes filled with tears.

I put my arms around her. "Why don't we sit down somewhere?"

"Oh, I'm sorry, I wasn't thinking. I don't seem able to stay put anyplace." She drew back from me and wiped her eyes with her fingertips.

"How can I help? Do you want to take a walk?"

She shook her head. "I should stay here in case Nick looks for me. He shouldn't have to wonder where I am. Let's sit in the dining room," she said. "I'll make some tea in a while."

You could hear the house's quiet. Why wasn't the phone ringing? People calling?

I followed Hedy and we settled at the dining-room table, where over the years I'd shared so many meals with Nick and Hedy that we'd lost count. They had painted the walls cranberry red, with glossy white woodwork, and hung a Tiffany lamp – a genuine one – over the round Mission oak table. The straight-backed chairs would have been hard and stiff but Hedy had tied soft cushions on them. An unmatched hutch, of maple, was cluttered with prizes from her collecting ventures, with odds and ends of cut crystal and china and silver, and no inch to spare.

As soon as we sat down Hedy's eyes filled with tears. "He was such a dear boy, this is killing me." She took a tissue from a Kleenex box on the table and rolled it into a ball. I noticed, then, several other tissue balls by her placemat.

"Do you want to talk about it? What happened with the police, I mean."

"I'd like this all to be a bad dream."

We sat silently for several minutes until she began again. "The police called around ten this morning, they'd been to Guy's after his landlady phoned them. She'd gone to an early Mass and stopped at the house on her way home. So we drove over at once. But everything happened so fast. They'd already taken his body to the morgue. We identified him there and they ordered an autopsy. It looks like he'd fallen and hit his head, in the back. It must have been a concussion. There was also a bruise on his forehead, it's hard to say why he fell."

"Could it have been a stroke? Or a heart attack? Young people have strokes too, we don't think of that."

"I don't know. I suppose that's why they want an autopsy. They asked if he was epileptic, if he might've had a seizure. But we said he never had a seizure in his life. He was very healthy."

"You're absolutely sure of that?"

"Of course I am." Her eyes narrowed. "What do you mean?"

"If he wasn't well, maybe he didn't want to worry you, maybe he kept it from…"

"There was nothing wrong with Guy, I'm sure of that. He was as healthy as he looked."

A mistake on my part. "I didn't mean to upset you, Hedy, I'm sorry…"

"Can you believe, they asked if he took drugs. They had the nerve to ask that. The police don't care. If it was a home invasion they'll never tell us, they don't want us to know. They'd rather pretend it was a drug overdose."

Her vehemence startled me, and for a moment I looked away. Nick had been leaning against the doorway, listening to us. I stood up and walked over to his side. "It's terrible," I said. "There are no words…"

He stared down at Hedy and finally said, "I didn't hear you come in."

Hedy took another tissue, blew her nose and sighed. "Do you want some tea?" she asked.

"I don't care," Nick replied.

Unlike Hedy, he'd changed from his street clothes to a navy blue velour bathrobe, his legs bare, with scuffed leather slippers on his black dress-socked feet.

"I'll make a pot anyway," she said. "You have to eat something, dear. You haven't eaten all day."

His arms hung at his sides, his hands shaking. "It doesn't matter."

"Yes, it does," I said. "Listen to Hedy."

"I can't talk now," he muttered. "I have to lie down."

"Do whatever you need to," I said.

Hedy began to cry again.

"He was our son." Nick shut his eyes and shook his head. "You have to excuse me."

Once he left us, Hedy put her hand to her forehead, rubbed her face hard, and then covered her mouth. I wouldn't have been surprised if she'd tried to bite her wrist.

I stood watching until she dropped her hand to the table, a limp appendage. She'd been trapped. "You can't give up now," I said.

"I told you, he's devastated," she said in little more than a whisper, and thought to add, "This is the end."

6

I spent the rest of the day at Nick and Hedy's, hoping I wasn't
in the way. Their telephone rang sporadically, and Hedy fielded
calls from the sofa, her feet propped up on a footstool. Often she
rubbed her knees with her free hand. Nick remained in his
room, and when I asked if I should go to him, she said, "Let him
be, he can't take it in." So I made a simple pasta for supper, with
garlic and olive oil, and Nick finally joined us. Now dressed in
jeans and a gray sweatshirt, he still wore his slippers. We ate in
silence.

After clearing the table, Hedy brought in the pie and another pot of hot tea, while Nick looked out the window blankly,
at a distant spot or memory.

Twilight had fallen, the blue hour, but you could still distin-
guish some features of their garden, one bush from another, in
the overall hazy blur. Nick may have been remembering a game
of croquet with the old set Hedy found at a yard sale, or tossing
a football with Guy, or teaching him how to ride a two-wheeler
– the things that fathers like to show their sons.

"I can take tomorrow off," I suggested. "For whatever you
need."

"We were always there for him," Nick said. "Remember how
he cried when we tore down the barn and put up the garage? I
had to convince him the car wanted a new place to sleep. He
loved that car."

Hedy pursed her lips. "Guy was seven that summer," she explained. "It was a big adjustment for him. With construction going on, and workers around, I didn't want him to wander too far from the house."

"I don't think he believed me, but he went along with it." Nick kept staring out the window.

"And he loved watching the garage go up," she said. "He always wanted to build things. I thought he would be an architect."

"He would have been a good one," Nick agreed. "I thought so too. We were there for him."

"He knew that," I concurred. Perhaps they hadn't heard my offer of help, and I didn't like to interrupt them by repeating it.

"Anything he wanted to do was fine with us," Hedy said. "As long as he really wanted it. We told him to follow his passion, that's what counts."

Nick looked desolately to his wife.

"It's what we believe," Hedy added. "It's who we are." She kept the conversation going for Nick's sake.

"Guy understood," I said, to support her. "His love of the Civil War…"

"I'm strung out." Nick suddenly blinked his eyes, as if to wake himself. "I don't know what I'm doing."

"Have some pie," Hedy coaxed. "It's apple."

"Apple," he repeated, almost questioning her.

Hedy's self-control amazed me. Somehow she managed to put her husband's pain before her own. One way of surviving? Or else she was still numb – that must be it.

"You don't have to do anything now," I said, wondering if I should ask about their plans for Guy's funeral. Given their beliefs, I couldn't imagine what the funeral might be. Yet any question would sound like prying.

Nick made no move to touch his plate.

"It must have been very hard, talking to everyone who called today," I remarked.

"I had to. But not any more. Not tonight." Hedy reached for the teapot and then drew back her hand without taking it. "Guy was too young to die," she said.

"Did you hear more from the police?" I asked.

"Nothing yet. Tomorrow they'll tell us about the autopsy, and when they can release the body. At least that's what they said this morning, but things could change. I don't know what to expect."

Nick raised his face and shook his head. "They're talking about our son like he's some kind of package."

"Guy will be cremated." Hedy looked directly at me. "That's what we'd want for ourselves, he knew that, and he wanted it, too. It was settled long ago."

"I want that, for myself."

"I didn't know," she said, surprised.

"We've never talked about this before."

"No, we never had to."

Nick appeared to lose interest in our exchange and began eating his pie, but he chewed a mouthful slowly as if he wasn't sure that he could swallow it. Then he set down his fork and looked back out the window.

"Are you okay?" I asked, immediately regretting my dull words.

"Why would I be okay? My son's dead. There's nothing to be okay about. Nothing can change that. Hedy's right, you know. Crime's up everywhere, there must've been a home invasion. Guy was brave, he would have stood up to them."

"We're exhausted," Hedy said. "But you've been so kind." She watched Nick for a moment, then added, "I think we need to meditate for a while."

I must have stayed too long. Nick now stared down at his unfinished dessert.

"We'll meditate a bit before going to bed, that's what we need."

We made the appropriate goodbye noises and I was on my way after promising to speak with them in the morning. The traffic on my trip home was light, with everyone apparently where they wanted to be on a Sunday night, and I arrived shortly after nine. Sheila had left two messages, and there was one from Theo, asking me to phone when I had the chance. I organized myself for the week ahead and left a message on a colleague's campus answering machine, saying that I wouldn't be at work the next day, something had come up. No details or explanation. I wanted to be free in case Hedy called.

The local television late news showed a quick camera shot of Guy's house, a longer one of the yard, and a panning shot down the block. While a sudden death like Guy's might not have caught network attention in a big city, Oberlin isn't Manhattan, not even Toledo or Cleveland, so newscasters here work with the principle of less is more, you go with what you have. The newsreader didn't mention a possible break-in, and no reporter had as yet obtained a photograph of Guy.

The next morning, after my first cup of coffee, I phoned Sheila.

"I left several messages," she said, a note of accusation in her voice.

"I got in late last night. I spent the day with Nick and Hedy."

She didn't inquire after them but immediately brought me up to date: "I already told you my mother knows Guy's landlady, Helen Wheeler, and she had a few things to say. She really liked Guy, she thought he'd be a good tenant. She never rents to young single women. She says they always have boyfriends overnight and it's like renting to a couple, they use more water and make more noise. Single guys go out for the night, they don't have girlfriends staying over."

"Well…" I began.

"You men have it so easy. Anyway, she liked Guy from the first. But it puzzled her that someone his age moved in with so little furniture. She'd wondered about his past, if he'd done time. Though landlords can't ask that. But she decided to take a chance on Guy."

"That was big of her."

"Do you want me to go on?"

"Sorry, Sheila. This is all pretty sad."

"Helen owns another house on the block, right across the street. She's had the same tenants there for five years, an older couple, so she asked them to keep an eye out, in case they saw anything strange."

"Okay…"

"So, after the police left she walked around the house. They'd sealed off the front door, but she didn't find anything suspect. No broken windows…"

"Hedy wondered about a home invasion. She mentioned that several times."

"The thought of that freaks me. Sometimes I worry about it."

"You've never said that before."

"I don't say a lot of things. But a woman alone has plenty on her mind, believe me. Every time Brad moved out I changed the locks."

As I recalled, he'd moved out at least three times in as many years.

"It makes me feel safer. So I buy a new lock. I can change them myself. Listen, did Hedy mention a funeral?"

"Nothing about that. Just a cremation."

"The poor kid. He was a sweetie. I wonder when we'll hear more?"

Sheila had a knack for reducing things to essentials, she wasn't big on nuance. But she meant well.

"After the autopsy," I guessed. "In a death like this it's required. Guy looked pretty healthy."

"He always looked sad to me."

"You thought that?"

"Something about his eyes. He was trying too hard to be cheerful. There's a big price for that. Would your friends hate it if I went to the funeral?"

"They know a lot of people, Sheila, and they must know you liked Guy. You'd be just one more person from the mall. I'm sure Claire Warren will come, you could sit with her."

I promised to keep Sheila posted, finished my coffee, and waited to hear from Hedy. But the morning passed without a call, and I felt foolish for taking the day off. Wanting a distraction, I flipped on the television news. Baby-boomers dressed up as Minutemen were waving placards somewhere, and shouting out protest, but at least the Antons didn't appear to be in the crowd. I turned off the television and for a while sat at the piano, playing through a couple of Bach fugues. Then, in a pile of old sheet music, I came across a piece I'd played with Hedy back in high school, Mendelssohn's "Song Without Words." I could almost hear the mournful tune, Hedy's cello soaring. Her parents had bought her a pretty good instrument, she didn't have to use one of the high-school's loaners, and I wondered if it she'd sold it, or just kept the cello out of the way. There was nothing in her home to suggest her youthful aspirations, as if she'd somehow erased her past.

Get a grip, I told myself. Stop wasting the day. I've known other deaths – all far more important in my life, of people I truly loved – but we don't choose the deaths that leave us troubled.

Of course, while I showered, Hedy left a message on my answering machine: "We haven't heard anything more, so I'm keeping my doctor's appointment this afternoon. Call when you have a chance. I'm very glad you came by yesterday, it meant a lot to us. More than you know."

Two

You kiss a beautiful mouth, and a key
Turns in the lock of your fear.

—RUMI

7

The coroner's report came in late on Tuesday afternoon, with no evidence of either a heart attack or a stroke. Guy had suffered two blows to his head, one in the back, the other on his forehead, and he died of a cranial bleed. The cause of his fall was unclear, with no evidence of drugs or alcohol, which his parents had already ruled out. Hedy told me all of this, and said that her son's body would be released to the undertaker. But the police intended to continue their investigation because the location of Guy's head wounds were an anomaly – people usually fell in one direction only. "That cop in charge," as Hedy referred to him, had shown little interest in her fears of a home invasion, but so far claimed to rule nothing out. Was there some sort of struggle? "Guy's my son," she said. "Don't they understand?"

The mention of drugs didn't surprise me. In the last few years there were several local busts, much covered by the papers, as if they were eager to mimic an episode of *Law and Order*. With the turn to warm weather, a few students had even become careless – or bolder – about smoking pot outside their rooms, and I'd had enough whiffs of it while walking about town to assume a thriving marijuana market.

What had Guy been doing with Neil that rainy night on the common? Buying a little pot, or selling some of his own stash? When he turned to look at me, Guy hadn't been pleased to see a familiar face, for a moment he'd looked embarrassed. Caught out. Was I imagining this? Surely it was an innocent meeting. Though he and Neil didn't appear to be strangers, perhaps they knew each other from the dental clinic. It was hard enough to see Guy as someone interested in drugs, let alone as a local drug lord. But, I reminded myself, I barely knew him.

Nothing further about Guy's death appeared in the newspapers, and I focused my attention on organizing a small exhibition at the library. Archival stuff, pretty esoteric, though doing it well mattered to me. Several days later I phoned my friends again. By now they must be planning the funeral. No answer, and their machine didn't pick up.

On Thursday, while eating a sandwich at my desk and riffling through papers, I received a call from Theo. He never phoned at work so it surprised me. "Neil's been arrested," he began, choking on the words. "The police were here this morning. Two of them. Big brutes. It was awful."

"Slow down, Theo. What happened?"

"They took Neil down to the station. For questioning."

"I don't think that's an arrest. What did they want?"

"To ask some questions. That's how they put it. We were finishing breakfast, we often have breakfast when he's working the late shift. I'd made oatmeal…"

"Theo, I don't need the menu. Questions about what?"

"That son of your friends. The ones at the antique mall."

As soon as he said the words, the sight of the two men leaning towards each other came back to mind. "How did Neil know Guy?"

Theo had never met Nick and Hedy, but they'd heard about each other. It's like that, sometimes. You keep friends separate when there's no reason to introduce them. When they wouldn't be a good fit.

"I don't want to talk about it over the phone. What if they're tapping the line?"

"Why would anyone do that?"

"How should I know? Can you come over? I don't know what to do. Should I be looking for a lawyer? And I haven't told you the latest about my house…"

"Hold tight till I get there. Right after work."

Though Theo and I lived only several blocks from each other, we spoke on the phone more often than we met. He jokingly called himself a confirmed agoraphobic and went out as little as possible. What he did all day I couldn't imagine, though he was devoted to the Turner Classic Movie channel and subscribed to at least a dozen magazines. He liked to quote a line from the comic Fran Lebowitz, who once quipped that when you leave your apartment you always risk being offended. We both liked that line.

Theo's two-storied brick house had been painted white for so many decades that it almost glowed with a mellow patina in the afternoon sun, and large coral azaleas seemed to preen under the bay windows. Inside, wherever one piece of furniture belonged, Theo managed to fit in two, like the display room of a high-end decorator. A three-foot-tall leather camel stood between two plaid wing chairs. Theo claimed that the camel brought back his childhood, when relatives sat around the dining-room table talking with his parents in Greek. As a boy he'd seen a picture of palm trees in Athens and assumed that camels must be nearby.

"Daphne's coming to spend the night," he said as soon as I stepped into the foyer. "I called her after I phoned you."

He must have been strung-out beyond himself. "Have you heard from Neil?"

"Nothing. Not a word. He's been gone for…" he looked at his watch, "for nine hours. I can't imagine what's taking so long."

"The police would want to talk to the last person who saw Guy alive. Maybe it was Neil."

I sat down on one of the plaid chairs and turned away from the camel. "Now tell me what happened. How did Neil know Guy?"

"They had a little affair. An affairette, you might call it."

"With Guy? You're kidding. Are you sure?"

"Neil came out to his wife, that's what their divorce is about. She wasn't pleased."

"You wouldn't expect her to be. Didn't they have children?"

"Two girls. In high school. Neil says his wife's a real ball-breaker. She wants everything. The house, alimony, child-care, his retirement. She's after every penny."

"But that has nothing to do with Guy. I didn't know he was…" I stopped. Hell, I should have guessed. Hedy and Nick would be horrified. None of us had cared enough to see. "How did they meet?"

"Neil never said. I think at a gym, though I can't say for sure."

"And you didn't ask?"

"I don't like to pry."

"C'mon, Theo. What did he tell you about Guy?"

"Very little." His tone of voice was tentative, almost abashed. This wasn't like a good celebrity breakup; it was, for him, too real. "I need a glass of wine," he said.

"Bring me one too, okay?"

Sun streamed in the bay windows, which lacked drapes or curtains or blinds. The tips of the azaleas, like blooms of fire, poked above the window sills. Beyond them, an expanse of green lawn spread out in manicured perfection. While Sheila was responsible for the flower beds, Theo had a lawn service spray the grass with every available pesticide.

When he returned with two cut-crystal goblets, heavy old-fashioned things, I said, "Now let's start again. This is really out of the blue. I didn't know about Guy."

"Like I said, Neil doesn't confide in me. That's how it is. I'm kind of surmising. His schedule at work changes a lot. He tells me, of course, he's very considerate. Until this week he was working days, now he's back on nights. Anyway, in the last month or so he's stayed out a couple nights. Two or three times."

I was certain Theo had an exact count and could even name the dates.

"Or came in so late I didn't hear him. I never ask questions, it's none of my business. He's renting a room until he gets on his feet, he doesn't owe me an explanation."

"So when did you hear about Guy?"

"On the weekend. The Sunday news, at six o'clock. We had the television on in the kitchen while I was making a salad, and when the reporter showed the house, Neil looked closer and said, 'I know him.'"

Theo has a television set in his kitchen, in the study, and in his bedroom, but not in the living room; he disapproved of televisions in living rooms.

"What else did he tell you?" I asked.

"Not much. That they'd seen each other a few times. I knew what he meant by the way he said 'seen.' I didn't think Neil was a eunuch, you know."

"It sounds like you had a rule of 'Don't ask, don't tell.'"

Theo looked down at his glass, didn't laugh, and I realized he'd yet to drink from it. "I'm pretty upset by all of this. I don't want the police questioning me."

"But you never met Guy. You didn't know him, did you?"

"Of course not. I've never laid eyes on him."

What an odd notion – to lay eyes on someone – as if sight were a tactile sensation. "Then you've nothing to worry about."

Theo grimaced. "I can't imagine Neil and Guy making it."

"You'll be fine, Theo. You'll get through this. Sheila's really upset about Guy."

"They're friends?"

"From the antique mall."

"Maybe that's where he met Neil. This change in life has thrown him."

Neil didn't seem the antiquing type to me. "If he came out to his wife he must've had some idea of what he was getting into. He didn't wake up one morning and say, 'From today on I'm going to sleep with men.'"

"He's probably bisexual," Theo said.

"I don't think you have the full story. What else did he say about Guy?"

"That he was new in town and didn't have many friends. And I think he said Guy was clingy."

"That's not a word I'd use for him, but we weren't close. Did Guy ever call here?"

Theo's eyes widened. "No," he said quickly, but added, "Neil has his own cell phone. He doesn't use mine."

I wondered if Theo was telling me the truth. I didn't ask if I could take a quick look at Neil's room, but it crossed my mind.

Clingy. Poor sweet Guy. Could be possible.

"Your friends' son should have found someone his own age. Neil's worried about his daughters. He told me he doesn't want to be involved with anyone now, he doesn't have time. His wife's poisoning the girls against him – he worries about them a lot. He's been a good father."

"You're taking his word for that."

"You have to trust people."

"That's what we've been taught."

We laughed and at the same time took swigs of wine. But it bothered me that Theo twice used the phrase "your friends' son" as if Guy didn't have a name.

The front door opened and a voice called, "Yoo-hoo, I'm here."

It was Daphne.

"Make way for supper," she announced. "I brought everything. I've got goodies."

We stood up as her footsteps crossed the hallway. She stopped at the entrance to the living room and said, "How are you I haven't seen you for a long time," in one breath.

Like her brother, Daphne was trim and conscious of her appearance, but she exuded nervous energy while his calm bordered on lethargy. There was more gray in her hair than I remembered, and it was now cut in a short bob with bangs that fell over her forehead. She wore a blue denim shirt waist, with gold hoop earrings, and gold bangles on her left wrist, which caught the light as she moved about.

"I'll get you some sherry," Theo offered.

"Oh, nice." She handed him two plastic bags. "There's a roast chicken in this one. Will you join us?" Daphne asked me. But before I replied, she looked at Theo. "Is Neil back?"

He shook his head.

"That's not good," she observed. "Not good at all." Turning to me, she crossed the room, sat down on the sofa and said, "Now tell me how you've been."

I mentioned my upcoming exhibition while she fluffed the velvet pillow beside her. "And you?"

"There aren't enough hours in the day. I told Theo I intended to use my retirement well, but some days I think it would be easier to have my job back."

Unlike her brother, Daphne was happy to leave her house, to volunteer as a docent at the botanical garden, join a book club, and sign up for night classes in Spanish – the list went on.

"You wouldn't think we're related, would you?" Theo joked on returning with Daphne's drink in a proper sherry glass. He held a bottle of wine in his free hand.

"I've heard about your friends' boy," Daphne said. "Theo told me everything. It's times like this that make me glad I never had children. They must be heartbroken."

"That's fair to say. Theo, what did you want to tell me about the house?"

"I'm not moving anywhere. Not yet. The couple's financing fell through. Who knows when I'll get another offer."

"It'll sell soon," Daphne assured him. "I have a good feeling." She turned to me. "Greeks have the sixth sense, you know."

"I wish I could phone the police station," said Theo, refilling our wine glasses. "I'd like to know what's happening."

"Oh, Theo." Daphne groaned. "That's a terrible idea. I won't let you do it, I forbid it."

Theo settled in his chair. "Whatever you say, Daph."

8

We are shadows – insubstantial, transient – and after we die, it's as if our shadows remain behind, lingering on, only now they're called ghosts. Or memories. Who was Guy? I asked myself that question many times in the following days. I wasn't sure why, but I felt the need to find out.

Neil returned from the police station while Theo and Daphne finished the meal she'd brought. I hadn't stayed for dinner, but Theo told me this the next day, relief in his voice. It appeared that a full investigation of Guy's death was underway. Theo even recalled that when the police came to his house they'd asked where Neil had been on Saturday evening, and Theo told them he'd been at home, in his room, and they'd watched *Saturday Night Live* together. Then I remembered a remark of Hedy's, that the pathologist's report suggested Guy had died more than fifteen hours before his body was found. Which suggested sometime Saturday afternoon, perhaps before supper. Watching late-night television with Theo didn't give Neil an alibi.

But Guy and Neil? Attraction – that funny old puzzle. It made no sense for a healthy young man to trouble himself over a middle-aged closet case. While I never understood Neil's charms, something about him drew out Theo's generosity. Would he lie for Neil? It didn't seem likely. Yet I'd never have expected him to rent a room to Neil, to anyone, in fact. And it took another leap to think of Guy and Neil as lovers. A drunken one-nighter, sure. But Guy didn't touch alcohol, and the autopsy had found none in his system. I saw only one reason for Neil's appeal: he was the guy next door. He could brag about his wife, his kids, the family's tomato plants or yellow Lab. He might have been the postman, the furnace repair man, the local bank manager. Easily overlooked, Neil threatened no one. And sometimes availability's the bottom line – Oberlin's not a big town.

It struck me that Guy's autopsy had taken longer than necessary, even for a body found on a Sunday morning. Considering his age, and the lack of an obvious cause of death, had the police been suspicious from the start? I could hardly ask Hedy. Or tell her what I'd learned at Theo's. An image of Guy's unlined open face appeared to me – that smile so eager to please – followed by his tentative laugh as he handed me a soft drink in his kitchen. I knew what I had to do. First, I'd phone Hedy.

"Nick's sleeping," she replied when I asked how they were. "Or trying to. He's been up all week. All hours."

It was just eight p.m., still early. "I hate to ask, but about the funeral plans…"

"There's not going to be a funeral."

"No funeral?"

"It's unnecessary. He was cremated yesterday. This is very difficult. Funerals are for the living, and his soul, well, he's already in another plane. That's our belief. But it's killing me. I gave birth to him, he knew life through me. A funeral won't bring him back."

Everybody still has to do something with their dead, but I wouldn't mention Guy's ashes. "If you're free this weekend…"

"Sunday might be good. I'll ask Nick."

We agreed to talk again soon, and then I phoned Theo. "Why don't you come for dinner tomorrow?" I suggested. "You and Neil."

"Tomorrow?" he hesitated, probably surprised that I'd include Neil in the invitation.

"Sure, it's the weekend. I'll enjoy cooking something."

"I was going to make…"

"Let me cook instead. You and Neil have had a rough week." I was about to say that we could put some steaks on the grill but remembered that Theo no longer ate red meat. "Is there anything Neil doesn't like?"

"He loves pasta. Any kind."

There's justice for you – skinny Neil's a pasta fan. "Is Daphne still with you?"

"No, she went home this morning."

That simplified things. "Check with Neil, okay? It'll be nice for you to get out. Both of you."

An hour later Theo called to confirm dinner. "And Neil says thanks. What can we bring?"

"Just good appetites."

The thought of Guy's ashes continued to trouble me, a young man reduced to little more than cinders. His picture now belonged on his dining-room bookshelf, along with the daguerreotypes of youthful dead soldiers, their open faces a rebuke to human stupidity.

On Saturday I shopped for dinner, straightened up the house, and made a quick pesto sauce. Since I rarely entertain any more, each chore reminded me of how reclusive I've become.

Theo and Neil arrived fifteen minutes late, or suitably on time, with a bottle of California red. I'd already set out a bowl of salted cashews, and offered drinks. Neil asked for a beer and Theo wanted wine, so I served them and poured a Scotch for myself. Down to business, but slowly at first. Neil might be wary. After a few words about my campus exhibition, which he'd heard of from the college security office, I asked for an update from Theo's real estate agent.

"I'm back to square one," he said, "but that's okay, though I wanted to be closer to Daphne."

Neil looked relieved. He had a good deal. When I'd phoned the other day Theo remarked, in passing, "I've got to get our laundry out of the dryer," and as soon as he said it, he took a gulp of air, as if to eat his words. Maid service, too.

"Daphne's cool," Neil said.

Cool – what a dumb word. And with no relation to Daphne.

We moved to the dining room. I brought out the food, and a plate of asparagus made its way around the table.

"You like to cook?" Neil asked.

"Not as much as I used to. But I like good food."

"I hate cooking," Theo chimed in. "If I could take a pill instead of eating, it would be fine with me."

"Not me," Neil said, spooning grated cheese over his pasta. "That would be awful. Food's about all I have left."

His silver-blond hair was cropped short to conceal a receding hairline, and his left ear had once been pierced, though he no longer had anything in the lobe. Like Guy, Neil had unusually white teeth, and lean, sinewy tanned arms, with his shirt sleeves rolled up to his elbows in a studied casual look. He resembled a mature model in a catalogue from L.L. Bean, the blue checks on his shirt matching the blue of his eyes.

"How did you meet Guy?" I took the plunge.

"Neil doesn't like talking about it," Theo said.

"I don't mind," Neil countered, twirling fettuccine around the prongs of his fork.

It was Theo who minded. Was he jealous?

"At the gym. Lifting weights."

"I've known his family for decades. His mother since high school, though it's hard to believe."

"Yeah, Guy said you were an old family friend."

"Are you interested in the Civil War too?"

"Huh?" He picked up a spear of asparagus and bit off the tip.

"Guy was a collector. Of war memorabilia."

Theo watched us, his empty fork in mid-air.

"Oh, that stuff. He said he'd tell me about it one day, but I never cared much for history. All those dates. But my girls like it. Can't think where they get it from."

"Your wife, maybe?"

He shook his head. "Not her. Neither of us."

"Guy loved history."

"I only saw him a couple times. That's what I told the police."

Neil didn't seem shy about discussing Guy. His encounter with the police must have frightened him out of his man-boy pose. Or was this more subdued Neil a performance?

"That night on the common, when it was raining…" I started to say, and realized from the way Theo leaned forward that he hadn't known about it.

"It's bad, what happened to him, but I don't know anything about it. I'll be frank with you, that's what you want. I knew it when Theo asked me to join you. We had sex a couple times, and he was more uptight than I am. There's not much else to say."

"Was he pestering you?" I asked. "I'm sure he meant it innocently."

"I told him not to get attached, I don't want strings. He phoned me a lot at work, on my cell, and I told him to stop. They don't like outside calls when you're on duty, and I need this job. I can't afford trouble."

"Everything's going to work out," Theo said.

"Guy seemed pretty upset that night. On the common. If you were trying to break off…"

"There was nothing to break off. It was all in his head." Neil set his fork down and looked me directly in the eye. "That's the last time I saw him. But I'm in a mess anyway. If my wife hears about this, her lawyer will go to town, and things are already bad enough."

"How did the police know about you?" I sounded like an inquisitor.

"Some neighbor of Guy's – some fuckin' busybody. She saw my car parked in his drive a couple times overnight and wrote down the license plate number. That's what the cops said."

Helen Wheeler's tenants. Reliable spies.

"It's a fuckin' police state, you never know who's watching you. And I don't need any trouble. I've never been a suspect before."

With a look of concern, Theo seemed about to burst into tears.

"They try to trip you up," Neil continued. "Yes, no, yes, no. They can make you say anything. They took my fingerprints like I was a bum. A criminal."

"I'm sorry," I said.

And I meant it.

9

Sunday, April 29

A long and troubling week and a half had passed since Guy's death, we were back in another stretch of unseasonably hot weather, and, as I opened the thick Sunday newspaper, I heard Sheila pull her SUV into my drive. Unannounced as usual. It was just nine o'clock, too early for company. At least I'd already showered and put on jeans and a clean T-shirt, as if I'd had a premonition.

Sheila waved to me through the kitchen window, but without a smile. She'd brought her mother along.

"I want to get an early start, before it's too hot," she explained when I joined them in the yard. "Mother wants to see your lilacs."

A row of old bushes ran across the back of my property, familiar standards and rarer specimens planted half a century ago by someone unknown to me. Their blooms were nearly finished, a few already browning at the edges, but their scent lingered over the garden.

The women walked across the grass together, Sheila striding purposefully.

"That's a Madame Felix!" Mrs. Carney exclaimed, at her own pace. She soon touched a white, single-petalled sprig. "One of the best whites."

"I didn't know," I said, following them, my *Times* left behind. "I just made coffee, if you'd like some."

"Not me," Sheila said. "I want to get started."

"It would be very nice, dear," Mrs. Carney said, adding, "I used to love it with sugar but my diabetes won't allow it anymore."

"I thought you were going to help me, Mother." Sheila carried a battered plastic pail with her tools and gardening gloves.

"First, we're having a little visit," replied Mrs. Carney, who wouldn't be cowed by her daughter. "You know I never turn down coffee."

Sheila often complained about her mother's disappointment in not having grandchildren. "She won't let go of it," Sheila would say, exasperated. "What am I supposed to do now?"

When I returned with two full mugs, we sat beside each other on the back porch steps. I imagined my paperback Aristotle waiting on the kitchen table. Ari – that great classifier, a man of categories – thought there were three reasons for friendship: usefulness, pleasure, and goodness. The first two, inevitably, have limitations, while pure goodness is rare. I would not ask myself which reason now worked in my garden; nothing's that simple.

At seventy-five, Mrs. Carney still made an effort to look after herself. Like her daughter, she wore jeans and a T-shirt, but her hair, which had turned white, was cut with care. She had on small pearl earrings, as if she'd started to get ready for church and changed her mind. She'd once owned a small greenhouse that supplied local florists with pots of violets, though the competition did her in long before I met her daughter. Business ran in the family, Sheila claimed, but not good luck.

"I suppose you've been following the Anton case," she began, watching her daughter kneel down to tie back some floppy daffodil leaves. "These cops are amateurs. Just hopeless. Once they decided Guy was gay, they probably lost interest."

The Anton case. Already named. "We don't know that for sure," I said.

"Well, he had male company overnight. That's what my friend Helen told me."

"We'll have to see what happens, Mrs. Carney."

"Now you've got to call me Doris. I'm sure I've asked you before. Just Doris, okay?"

"Are you talking about Guy?" Sheila called.

"Of course, dear," her mother answered. "What else?" Then Doris turned to me. "There's no public interest, that's the problem. If he'd been abducted…"

"Anything break yet?" Sheila called.

"Guy died of a concussion," I said. "My friends called it a cranial bleed, that's what the coroner reported. He fell and had a fatal concussion."

"Has there been an inquest yet?" Doris asked. "I didn't read about one in the papers. If there's no inquest, the case is still open."

"Mother watches all the TV crime shows, don't you, Mom? You live for them."

"Never mind, smartie. You don't expect me to watch those silly news programs – all those people yelling at each other." Doris paused before whispering, "She's in a bad mood."

"What's that, Ma?"

"We're just visiting, dear. You go on with your work." She lowered her voice. "The police ought to have an angle by now, I know that much."

And there had to be an inquest, she was right. To look at evidence and close a case. My thoughts stopped short: *a case.* I'd used the term, too.

The clear, bright morning sky augured well for the day. A good day to drive over to Nick and Hedy's. I wondered if they knew that the police had questioned Neil, or if they'd heard about Neil at all. A shock, it would have been. Occasionally they'd mentioned that Guy said it was difficult to meet decent companions, *decent* was their word, though he might have used it. Party girls or troubled divorcees, they made up the field.

"That overnight fellow, I wonder if they found him yet?" Doris mused.

No reply from me. Though I had little reason to protect Neil, his name would be all over town if I mentioned it. And maybe Guy had another nighttime buddy.

"He was there the day your friends' son died. Her tenants saw him, in the afternoon."

Sheila came up to the porch stairs. "I need a glass of water." She stepped around us, towards the back door. "Don't move, I'll get it myself."

"On Sunday, Doris?" She'd caught my attention.

"No. Saturday afternoon. That's what they told the police. They were out on their porch, just back from grocery shopping."

At dinner, Neil said that the last time he'd seen Guy was the rainy night when I ran into them on Tappan Square. If I closed my eyes, the two men leaning toward each other were as clear as anything in my garden.

The kitchen door slammed shut and Sheila joined us. "I want a breather."

"You work too hard," Doris observed. "You're like me."

Sheila sat on the bottom step and took a gulp of water. My backyard faced east, and the sun was already hot on our faces. Neil hadn't mentioned visiting Guy in the afternoon. What had he told the police?

"The cops were at the mall yesterday," Sheila said between sips. "Asking about Guy."

"What would his death have to do with the mall?"

"He hung out there a lot, looking after his parents' booth. And everyone knew about his Civil War collection." She took another gulp and frowned.

"Sheila's had a break-in," Doris said. "Somebody smashed her backdoor lock."

"Let me tell it, Mother," Sheila cut her off. "On Friday afternoon, while I was working. But they didn't get much. I always keep a few cheap gold chains in my jewelry box, as a decoy. I'm sure it was Loretta, but how to convince the police? Now if I was a rich professor, you can imagine how high they'd jump. I don't own rubies and emeralds…"

"Neither do most people at the college."

"They're rich enough. And it had to be Loretta." She glared at me as if I'd been Loretta's sidekick. "She keeps calling in the middle of the night."

"You're still getting those calls?"

"Almost every night, I told you she's crazy. She's probably jealous of me, because of Brad."

"He must be enjoying this," Doris observed.

"I don't know," Sheila said, ready to defend him.

"What are you going to do?" I asked.

"Will you come by and change the message on my answering machine? If a man's voice says 'Leave us a message' it might put her off. Last night I told Brad to make her stop. I love him but he's practically brain dead."

"Now dear," Doris interjected.

"Mother, you know I can't talk about Brad with you."

"And the police?" I asked.

"They took some fingerprints and offered to give me the name of a locksmith. Can you believe it? Like I couldn't put in a new lock myself."

10

"You should know…" Hedy began, and then stopped to take a deep breath. "We wanted you to know…" she stopped again.

I gripped my phone, the effort in her voice alarming me. I'd just gotten home from work and surveyed the fridge. It was one of those times when a sandwich would have to do.

"Nick spent the night in the hospital."

"What happened? Where is he now?"

"At home. Back at home. Last night he had terrible chest pains, like a heart attack. He didn't want to go to the hospital – it was after ten and he just wanted to go to bed. It's hard to know what's best, but I've got to take care of him. So I called 911 for an ambulance."

She took another long breath.

"And then?"

"They kept him overnight. For observation. They did an EKG and all the blood work. His father died young, at forty, from a heart attack. It's in his family."

"Was it a heart attack, Hedy?"

"No, they said it was stress."

"That's good."

"Stress can be a killer, too," she contradicted.

"I only meant it's good he didn't have a heart attack. You made the right decision."

"I don't know what I'd do without Nick. It was terrible, he was in such pain. He thought his chest was going to split in half."

Too often I find myself left with only empty words. "You'll help him," I offered. "You always do."

"I've got to. Since Guy died nothing's been the same. I can't sleep, but I have to force myself to get out of bed in the morning."

"Is it alright if I drive over tonight? After supper, for a short visit. I'd like to see Nick."

"That would be good."

I finished in the kitchen and headed out. The pleasant May evening, along with some Brahms on the radio, almost distracted me during the drive. I tried not to imagine what I'd find at my friends'. I could see Hedy's face tight with fear, and hear it in her voice. She'd made no effort to conceal her distress.

As soon as I reached their front door, it opened with Hedy standing behind it. "We've been waiting," she said.

"The traffic was heavy. How's Nick doing?"

"It's been a bad day."

"What an understatement," said Nick, joining us in the hallway. He rested a hand on Hedy's shoulder. It had been more than a week since our last meeting and he'd obviously lost weight, his face haggard with grief.

"But you didn't have a heart attack," I said, alarmed by his appearance.

"No, I was spared that."

I followed them into their living room, where Nick settled in his leather recliner, Hedy chose a corner of the sofa closest to him, and I sat in the opposite chair. A glass vase of purple tulips drooped their heads toward the top of the coffee table between us. Funny, the things we remember. Somewhere I'd read that

Georgia O'Keeffe claimed to love tulips because they died so beautifully.

"What did the doctors tell you?" I asked.

"Not much. But you won't guess that from their bills."

Hedy concurred with a nod. She'd put on bright lipstick and the blue eye shadow Nick liked, as if to reassure him that all was well, but her face appeared sunken underneath the mask.

"I wasn't an interesting case. They gave me some sleeping pills," he added.

"You've lost weight," I said.

"We don't feel like eating," Hedy said. "This morning I forced down a banana. It was all I could face."

"His ashes are over there," Nick said, gesturing at an ornately carved console table, one of Hedy's estate-sale finds, beside my chair. "We brought him home Monday."

I turned to see an unopened cardboard box, perhaps a foot square, almost at eye level with me. It was sealed with several wide strips of clear tape.

"We can't open the box." Hedy pursed her lips. "It was hard enough bringing him home."

Nick stared at me without any expression.

I glanced back at the box. No one would have guessed its contents – it might have been any of the parcels Nick made for Hedy's eBay sales. Somewhere across the country an anxious customer might have been waiting for it. The notion made me flinch.

"What've you heard from the police?" I asked tentatively.

"Nothing since the inquest."

"I didn't know there was one already. I would have gone with you."

"It's not a formal hearing, only the coroner's verdict," she said. "We read it on Friday. It was horrible, all the details. Ohio coroners have to be physicians – that's not true everywhere – and he was so thorough, I can't bear thinking about it."

Without a word between them, Hedy had taken over the conversation. Nick cleared his throat and then reached out to turn on the reading lamp at his side. A pool of silvery light enveloped him.

"It hasn't been in the papers."

Hedy sighed. "No? I didn't look. They said 'manner of death undetermined' – that's it. No one knows what happened."

My question about the police was thoughtless. What suffering person likes hearing another's curiosity? Hedy didn't mention Neil Breuler, although the police may not have brought him up. Again, I saw Guy on the common, grasping his bicycle while Neil leaned toward him. Guy had always seemed lost in the daydreams of adolescence. I must have recognized that he dreaded being different, yet I never said a word of assurance. When did I first attach "poor" to "Guy" as if the words belonged together? Before he joined the army? After he returned home? I couldn't remember.

"We've got to empty his house by the end of the month," Hedy said. She bent over suddenly, picked up a tulip petal that had fallen to the table and cupped it in her hand. "It's what his landlady wants."

"I can't do it." Nick shook his head. He pulled a lever on his chair and, with a sharp snap, a footrest pushed his feet upward.

"His rent's only paid until the end of the month, dear. We still have…"

"Let me help you," I said.

They looked to each other, startled at first, or so it seemed.

"I can put his things in boxes, I can even bring boxes from the library. There's no reason for you to torture yourselves."

"It's very kind of you," Hedy said finally, looking down at the petal, studying it as if to fix its color in her memory.

"That is kind," Nick said. "We might take you up on the offer."

"I really mean it. I can't imagine what you're going through but there's no reason for you to spend a minute in that house."

"We know you mean it. I'm glad you came by."

Of course I didn't tell them that I'd had a phone call from Claire Warren asking if I knew anything more about Guy's Beecher Stowe letters. "Life has to go on," she'd opined. I should have said, "But not yet. Not so fast."

"Would you like some tea?" Hedy asked. With a nervous movement of her fingers she crushed the petal.

"I don't want anything," Nick said somberly.

Earlier that evening, when I'd talked with Hedy on the phone, Nick must have been out of the room. She'd spoken more easily and reminded me that after Nick inherited his uncle's auto dealership, he'd hated the business and become withdrawn, despondent. "He's already had one nervous break-down," she'd confided. "I can't let him have another. He was very sick then. I have to be careful, that's how it is. I know how to take care of him."

Such an old-fashioned term, nervous breakdown. Almost genteel, Victorian.

"I think we should have some tea," she insisted.

"Whatever you say." Nick looked at her intently. Shadows from the lamp light fell over his face, darkening it. He sat immobile, his hands folded together. Was he recalling his own father's death, back when Nick was ten? Still a boy, who had to grow up without a father. And now he'd lost his son, his only child.

Instead of moving, Hedy kept her focus on her husband. "I want us to have some tea."

"I just want to sleep," he replied testily.

"I know that, dear, I know that," she repeated.

Their trip to the hospital had scared them both and wouldn't be easily forgotten. Not at our age, not now. Looking at the oil painting above the sofa, an impressionistic cluster of peonies – another of Hedy's finds – I wished they would tell me about their visit from the police. Guy had been dead for twelve days, his body had been cremated, his ashes brought home, to the console table beside me, yet the nature of his death remained unclear.

"I can pack up Guy's things any time you like," I offered once more, thinking I should leave soon.

"I can't believe this was Guy's karma," Hedy said. "He never harmed anyone."

Nick listened without appearing to take in her words. He must have been remembering the hospital, the doctors, their tests.

"I don't believe in destiny," I said.

Hedy put her hand to her forehead, as if to stop herself from falling. Before I knew what was happening she leaned forward and began to sob. Her shoulders heaved as she shook back and forth while she gasped for air. Sweat suddenly beaded her face.

I moved to join her but Nick said, "Let me."

In an instant he sat beside Hedy and she dropped her head against his chest, where she continued to weep.

Nick rocked her in his arms, his head bowed over hers. "I'm here," he said softly, stroking her head. They held on to each other as I watched. Helpless, I stayed in my chair.

In time Hedy pulled away and wiped her cheeks with one hand. "I'm sorry, I can't take it. I want to be stronger, but he was my son."

"There's nothing to be sorry for," I said.

Nick drew her back again and she laid her face on his chest. "I'm here, hon," he said, at the same time closing his eyes. "I'm here for you."

By ten o'clock I drove into my garage and locked the car. Of course the thought of Nick and Hedy had shadowed me home. It's horrible to admit but Guy's death had put a stop to their rants, and it was a relief. They'd been subdued by loss, and the need to mollify them was no longer uppermost in my mind. While watching them tonight I remembered how Hedy's voice had dropped to a whisper when she'd mentioned Nick's earlier breakdown. That auto dealership must have ended Nick's dream of a poet's life, as if his talent hadn't panned out and he'd failed himself. How much disappointment can anyone live with?

Since I rarely saw Nick apart from Hedy, there was little opportunity for confidences. Once or twice he'd mentioned their first meeting, at a crafts fair on the common. Their court-ship was a short one, that much I knew. Occasionally Nick referred to his "difficult" mother, who blamed Hedy for his unfinished doctorate. Apparently her idea of a professor son didn't include his beautiful young wife. Hedy's parents had died in a car crash when she was in her twenties, so my friends had to contend with only one living in-law, yet Hedy claimed she'd always felt like an intruder at family dinners. This made no sense; Hedy should have been a splendid daughter-in-law, inter-esting and thoughtful. But people can hurt each other without meaning to.

And now they were locked in a grief that nothing would alter. Neither Hedy nor Nick had mentioned what the police still wanted. Sheila said that two cops had been at the mall ask-ing about Guy. I'd like to have heard their chatter, listened in to their suspicions.

Without stopping to check my answering machine, I climbed into bed. Some days the best thing to do is turn out the lights and hope for sleep. But restless, I picked up Aristotle. At least he might slow my thoughts down.

I flipped through his first essay on friendship, refreshing my memory before turning to the second. The section headings caught my attention, especially the one marked, "Occasions of breaking off friendships." Though it seemed like a betrayal, I began reading: "Another question that arises is whether friendships should or should not be broken off when the other party does not remain the same." I read that sentence twice, stopping each time at "when the other party *does not remain the same.*"

According to Ari, friendships based on utility or pleasure are easily set aside, and this is normal in the course of life. "But if one accepts another man as good, and he turns out badly and is seen to do so, must one still love him?" Now this question was more than I was ready to face. Not tonight, after leaving Nick and Hedy in their pain. So I set the book down, back in its place on the bedside table.

"...*when the other party does not remain the same.*"

My head kept churning. What would Ari think about a change in political values? Yet I hesitate to use the word *political* here, as if I'd been having reasonable debates with the Antons. All sides to an argument aren't equal, some are better than others. Aristotle, at least, understood the word *better* – you might say he thrived on it.

Before I left Nick and Hedy, we'd finally had our tea, as she insisted. "I've been thinking," she'd said, setting a tray of hot mugs on the coffee table. She almost knocked over the vase of tulips and I held my breath for her. "If you're really willing to pack Guy's things, it would be a great help."

"If you're sure?" Nick asked. "It's an imposition."

"No, it's not. It's the least I can do. I remember Guy's place – I told you he showed me around. It won't take more than a morning."

Hedy poured milk in all of our mugs and handed one to Nick. I didn't remind her that I liked my tea clear.

"When did you start sculpting badgers? The one on Guy's mantel was great."

A safe topic, badgers. Though aren't they one of the few animals who kill not only for food but also for pleasure?

"You liked it?" Her eyes widened.

"Very much."

"Then you should keep it. Please, take it with you."

"Oh, Hedy, no. You made it for Guy."

"I couldn't face having it here. It's yours now. That way you'll always remember Guy."

Thinking back over my evening, I readjusted my pillow, tossed about, and stared at the alarm clock as its digital numbers flipped by. They kept to their proper order, but I imagined the numbers jumping randomly, from 11:30 to 11:17 to 12:05 – a clock where time was as unpredictable as life. Since Guy's death, Hedy said, she had to force herself to get out of bed every morning, daylight no longer an ally.

Annoyed with myself, I went to open a window, hoping fresh air might help. The street outside was perfectly still. I leaned against the sill and enjoyed the dark quiet night. How, I wondered, had Aristotle answered his question about the responsibilities of friendship? So much depended on what one meant by the phrase "a good man." Could a good person, for instance, hold obnoxious views? Probably not. And if those views were set in stone, what then?

I returned to bed, sitting on its edge, and switched on the night-table lamp. Ari was waiting patiently, so I read his answer: "Surely it is impossible, since not everything can be loved, but only what is good." The rest of the paragraph appeared to be an elaboration of that position. I set the book aside again.

Hedy's image remained, unshakeable, before my eyes. When she'd handed me the key to Guy's house, she'd paused for a moment before saying, "There's just one thing…"

"What's that?"

"Don't ask Sheila to help you. I don't want her snooping through my son's things."

11

Tuesday, May 8

The final weeks of the academic year hint at the beginning of summer in the library. Meetings about fund raising, visits to alumni donors, and writing a conference paper, such tasks were ahead, along with the annual budget talk. Overnight, it seemed, fewer students remained in the stacks until closing hours. So far this spring I'd seen only three of them asleep in study carrels.

My office, a utilitarian spot, is impersonal: no private photographs or mementos. One predecessor left behind a large framed brass rubbing of a medieval knight, and I kept it in place because the image suits my job as a protector of old papers. I've even joked to an occasional visitor that he's my double. I was looking through some book orders when a sharp knock on my half-open door caught my ear. Neil Breuler stood there in his security-guard jacket. "Can I talk to you?" he asked.

Since Neil had never come to my office before, his presence surprised me.

"Sure, come in. Has something happened? The library's been pretty quiet today. Are there more swastikas?" I hoped February's ugliness wasn't returning.

"I'm on my lunch hour," he began, without moving, as if to reassure me that he wasn't wasting the college's time. "It's about your friend's son."

"You can shut the door," I suggested.

"I've been pretty worried. But I don't like to talk about it with Theo. You know how depressed he gets, and that only makes things harder. He doesn't know I'm here to see you, I didn't tell him." Neil headed to a chair. "If the police are checking alibis, that must mean there's a crime."

"Not necessarily. They're looking for leads and probably don't have any. But they have to investigate somehow."

"Have you heard anything from your friends?"

"Nothing. They're wondering too. But charges haven't been laid, or we'd have read about that."

Neil slumped, expressionless. Sleekly modern, the chair wasn't particularly comfortable.

"When the police questioned you, why did they keep you so long?"

"I waited a couple hours before anyone even spoke to me, and then the detective disappeared, I think he went to lunch. They drag things out. Then they kept asking if I had any idea why someone would harm Guy, or who might have a reason."

"When did you see Guy last? It wasn't that night on the common."

"Not exactly." He looked embarrassed. "We went back to his place that night. I knew I shouldn't have, but, hell, sometimes I don't think right. My ex calls me a 'total washout,' that's what she says. And in front of our kids. Anyway, I'd decided not to see Guy again but he convinced me to go home with him. Maybe he thought he could talk me out of it. That was the last time we were together. But on Saturday afternoon I drove to his place to say it was over, we couldn't see each other anymore. I figured he got the wrong impression after Thursday – he'd left several messages on my cell. Thursday was a mistake."

"So you were there on Saturday afternoon. Look, I don't mean to sound like a cop."

Neil bent forward, hands resting on his knees. Light from the sun-filled window behind him caused his features to blur and darken. Inertia seemed to have overtaken him. Of course he had no reason to trust me.

"About four. I rang the bell several times but he didn't answer. He wasn't expecting me, I didn't call first, it was sort of spur of the moment, you know. The place was locked up, like he wasn't around."

"He may have already fallen. Did you tell the police about Saturday?"

"I had to. What with those neighbors watching every move on the street."

Yes, the neighbors. In a small town like Oberlin people know each other's business even when they don't know each other. "But you didn't mention this when we had dinner."

"Not in front of Theo. It would've upset him."

We were all protecting Theo from himself.

"And there's another thing. I don't like to bring it up, maybe it'll sound crazy, but one night at Guy's I was looking out the front window and I swore I saw Theo's car driving by."

This I hadn't expected. "All black cars look pretty much the same in the dark."

"Not if you know cars," he replied.

We stared at each other for a moment. "Well, I suppose you couldn't ask him about it," I conceded.

"Hell, no."

"It might have been your imagination."

"That's what I told myself. But I think he's looked through stuff in my room, too. You won't mention any of this to him?"

"Of course not."

"I'm just spooked by everything."

"But you had no motive to harm Guy, did you?"

"Hardly," he said. His voice had suddenly deepened.

"I'm sorry, Neil, I'm not accusing you of anything."

"Maybe I shouldn't have come here. What motive…"

"Well, if he was a threat to your divorce. The other night you said he could make trouble. The police might have thought Guy was going to speak to your wife…"

"I worried about that myself," he interrupted. "But Guy didn't threaten me, he never said anything like that. His feelings were pretty bottled up. Yet people believe what they want to, and they'll always believe the worst. I wasn't Guy's first, you know," he said defensively.

"I don't know very much about Guy or his life."

"Neither do I. We met at the gym. Over in Amherst. Where my family lives."

A ten-mile drive from Oberlin, Amherst has a population similar to ours, but the town is more spread out, and with more retail shopping.

"It's a new gym, and pretty clean," he continued. "I don't like to discuss things like this in front of Theo, he's kind of possessive. Maybe I shouldn't say that. He's curious yet I don't think he likes hearing…"

"I know what you mean. But what about Guy?"

"Before we met he had a fling with someone else from the gym. Older and married, like me. Guy likes them married, though he wouldn't admit it."

"He told you this?"

"Yeah, well, some of it. But I could see for myself. He was always hanging around this other guy. Maybe I shouldn't say…" he hesitated.

"Look, I'm certainly not going to tell Guy's family. Or Theo."

"His name's Ray Hatchard. He's a high-school football coach. Married, with three kids. It's funny, he has three girls and I have two."

With the choices Guy made, he never had a chance at feeling good about himself.

"He even warned me about Guy the first time he saw us talking at the gym."

"Warned you?"

"Yeah, he said Guy was too serious, that's what I remember. Ray's bisexual. Like me. I like women, too."

"And Guy?"

"Who knows? I don't think he did. Whatever went on between them lasted about half a year, Guy told me that. But frankly I wasn't interested, his talk made me uncomfortable. Guy wanted to be a couple with someone, so I told him he was looking in the wrong place. Maybe this will sound odd but sometimes he reminded me of my girls, the way he talked about having someone special…"

"Was Guy out at the gym?"

"No, not like that. It's a closety place. But things happen."

I could imagine. Horny married men bored with their wives, younger men looking for a hookup, a little cash passing between them, or maybe not. "Did you pay him?" I asked.

"God, no, never. Is that what you think of me?"

"I'm just trying to see this from every perspective. Isn't that why you came here?"

"I'm pretty confused," he said in a forlorn voice. "I didn't know where else to go, that's how confused I am." He gave me a wounded little-boy smile, and maybe it was genuine.

"Were there others? Before you and Ray?"

Neil shrugged. "Something happened when he was in the army. I didn't ask a lot of questions, you know. An officer came onto Guy, I never got the whole story. I don't even know how long ago…"

"Guy enlisted right after high school."

"I don't remember what he said. But he went a long time without any sex, he told me that. I didn't want to hear about Guy's past. And I'm not much of a talker."

"You're doing fine," I said, aware that I was prompting him. So far he didn't seem to mind.

"You're okay, that's what Theo says. If you're interested in something he says you're like a dog with a bone."

"Did you tell the police about Ray?"

"No. Was that wrong?" He kept that crooked smile on his face, a smile made of both shame and defiance.

"It would have given them another lead."

"Shit." Neil gazed at the floor, avoiding eye contact. "I really blew it."

"It probably wouldn't have made a difference."

He raised his head and looked around my office. "It's nice here. Nice and bright. And that poster's cool. Is it from a movie?"

"It's a brass rubbing. I like it, too."

When Neil stood up to leave it was as if he had to submit to his fate. He thrust a hand out towards me and I clasped his, our shake a bond, if not allegiance. I'd given my word to be discreet. "Better get back to work," he said. "Before they miss me."

My afternoon meetings were a distraction from Neil's visit, yet his words lingered. If he hadn't been truthful, why bother? I thought of looking up Ray Hatchard's telephone number, not to call him but just for something to do. Butt out, I told myself. I couldn't help Neil, couldn't offer an alibi. And I was only a little closer to understanding Guy. Yet Neil was wrong. There was nothing adolescent about Guy's desire for love, like a teenage crush. I recalled myself at Guy's age. The details aren't important, we've all had a first love. The longing and joy and elation, Guy wanted his share. Who could blame him?

When I got home that night I went straight to the kitchen and took out the leftover lamb curry from the weekend. I never mind eating the same thing several nights in a row, not when I like it. I poured my Scotch, ignoring the bleeping light on my answering machine. Instead, I turned on the radio, bypassing the news for a station that was devoting an hour to Artie Shaw recordings, big band music about as far away from my life as you could get. This was my parents' music, and I recalled their old 78s. Then my thoughts returned to Guy and Neil. I should have asked if he'd spoken with this Ray fellow after Guy's death, or what the other hawks at the gym had to say about it. With questions piling up I tried to focus on "Perfidia" while enjoying my drink, but Neil's visit nagged away.

So I picked up my copy of Aristotle, left on the kitchen table, and thumbed through his second essay on friendship. Goodwill, he wrote, may be part of friendship but they're not the same thing. Ari used the phrase "inactive friendship" for it, which makes sense. I didn't have to be Neil's friend, or Guy's, to extend goodwill. More interesting was the question Aristotle went on to pose: "Why does the happy man need friends?" Since he defines happiness as an activity – the condition of being active – it follows that happiness involves other people, and friends become desirable. Yet he ends with a reminder that the friendship of "bad men" is not only undesirable but "evil" while the friendship of "good men" is in itself "good." No relativist, Ari, he never had a postmodern emotion. Using his terms, were Neil and Guy good or bad men? At the risk of sounding mid-Victorian, neither of them gave much thought to marriage vows. We're so used to explaining people psychologically, by some personality disorder – they're narcissistic or depressive or compulsive or passive aggressive, or just plain crazy – that the question itself seems antique, like a dusty object at Hedy's booth in the mall. I put down the book for now. I didn't want to burn the rice.

Later, after clearing up the kitchen, I listened to my messages. Theo had left two, and his voice sounded eager for a chat. It was just after eight when I reached him.

"You're always doing so many things," he said. "I don't know how you find the energy."

"Multiple vitamins," I said. "What's going on, Theo?"

"Did Neil call you?"

"No, he didn't call me." I hated to break Neil's confidence. Maybe Ari would consider it goodwill. "Why would you think he'd phone me?"

The words *call* and *phone* were heavy on my tongue. Though I remembered Neil's idea that Theo had followed him to Guy's, there was no way of bringing it up without admitting to our visit.

"Yesterday, after dinner, I went into the kitchen to clean up and Neil was sitting at the table with my address book open in front of him."

"And?"

"To your page."

"You mean the one with my number? What did he say?"

"I pretended not to notice, I just went over to the sink."

"But he must have seen you."

"He pushed the book aside like it was in his way. I wasn't going to accuse him of anything, maybe I'd left the book open."

"You can recite my phone number in your sleep, you weren't looking it up. Are you telling me everything, Theo?"

"Of course, Chief."

"Chief" was Theo's nickname for me. He used it when he felt irritated or impatient or frightened.

"What are you worried about?" I asked.

"Oh, nothing. I just worry too much, you know that."

12

My turn of the key opened the front door to Guy's house, and a musty smell hit me. The blinds had been shut tight and dust particles swam about in the living room's closed-in air. I wondered if Guy's neighbors across the street were watching. By now they might have copied down the number of my car's license plate. I'd already piled boxes from the library on the front porch, some filled with newspaper and bubble wrap. It was ten o'clock, later than I'd hoped to start.

First things first: a walk-through to see what needed packing. I remembered the rooms well enough and nothing much had changed – a hand-knit afghan now tossed over the back of Guy's recliner, the dining-room shelves a little fuller with books. I didn't know exactly what I was looking for but I was looking for something.

Guy's bedroom had only the most basic furniture: a maple chest of drawers and matching night table, probably from his childhood, and a new king-size bed. No pictures on the walls, no carpet on the hardwood floors, and on the top of the bureau only a few coins and a key ring. On the bedside table, however, an old leather-bound book. I reached for it and was surprised by a volume of poems by Rumi, with this inscription: *"Happy Birthday, Love, Mom and Dad"* in Hedy's flamboyant hand, but no year. There was no lamp on the night table, as if Guy never read in bed. Then I noticed the open closet door. His clothes were neatly lined up, along with his shoes: three pairs of runners and some black loafers. I would bag all the clothes for Goodwill, as Hedy suggested when we spoke last night. Though Neil had slept here with Guy, or spent time on the bed, the room seemed almost monastic.

In the bathroom, a navy blue towel hung over the shower bar. While most of the white tiles had grayed with age, Guy kept the place immaculate. His electric shaver remained in place and a red tooth brush hung in a holder by the sink, a tube of Crest beneath it. The medicine cabinet held only a roll-on deodorant and a new tube of KY lubricant. I tossed everything but the shaver into a garbage bag. On top of the toilet tank sat a well-thumbed copy of Ayn Rand's *Atlas Shrugged*, and I remembered reading her *Fountainhead* when I was fourteen – a great book to grow out of. Guy probably didn't know that Rand was also famous for greeting her young lover naked under a mink coat.

Now face the basement, I told myself. Where Guy had died.

First, I stopped in the kitchen. The cupboards that Sheila had painted held only a few packs of vegetable cubes, some cans of black beans, packages of dried pasta – the whole-wheat variety – and a dozen jars of spices. Hedy hadn't said anything about the food but I doubted that she'd want it. Goodwill probably wouldn't, either. The kettle I gave Guy sat on the sink, beside a cheap white plastic toaster.

Finally, I flipped on the light at the top of the basement stairs. They felt solid enough as I headed down, trying not to imagine Guy at the bottom. He must have died without a will – who has a will at thirty-four? Not a young single man starting out on his own.

For an older bungalow, the basement seemed dry. Its walls had been painted a celery green, but gray damp spots ran along their base where they met the floor. Guy's big rolltop desk – the desk he was so proud of – had a scattering of papers over it. My footsteps echoed on the cement floor behind me. Had I locked the upstairs front door after coming in? The basement made me shiver. Freud has an essay called "The Uncanny," written right after the First World War. It's about death and ghosts and revenants, the things that give us the creeps. I was glad to think of it now. Even Freud sometimes got the creeps.

Since there was no obvious cause of death, what had happened in this basement? Guy wasn't epileptic, he didn't have a seizure. And the wooden handrail beside the stairs felt secure to my hand, he shouldn't have lost his step.

I looked about slowly. The basement was made up of two spaces. I stood in the first of them, a small area with old wall shelves painted the same celery green, and Guy's office furniture: his desk, a chair, and a battered metal filing cabinet with three drawers. A doorway, minus the door, led into the furnace room, with a sink to one side. No washer or dryer. I walked towards the darker room and saw that its windows had been painted over. The cracked white paint appeared to be ancient.

Where had Guy's landlady found his body? Sheila hadn't mentioned it, nor had Hedy or Nick, and I hadn't thought to ask. "In the basement," that's all anyone said. No one had suggested he'd fallen down the stairs, so his body might have been near the desk. I stared at the cement floor, long ago painted dark gray.

Was it possible that someone had pushed Guy? Maybe that's what the police thought.

The chair at Guy's desk hadn't been moved back under it. I leaned over and picked up some papers. One photocopied sheet announced a "Civil War Encampment" at the James A. Garfield National Historic Site on Saturday, July 11. "Free Admission!" it proclaimed, above a list of activities. Re-enactment units would march, drill and fire weapons, and there would be a scavenger hunt – for what? – with music from the Camp Chase Fifes and Drums, a diorama of the Battle of Middle Creek, and even "a living history presentation of General Robert E. Lee." Easy to imagine the crowds shoving and spilling pop and calling out at the top of their voices.

The bottom of the sheet read "To Arms! To Arms!" and urged children ages five to twelve to volunteer for the Mini Militia, where they could drill with a toy Civil War rifle.

More posters, all photocopies, announced similar events across the state. Was that how Guy planned to spend his summer, going from one Civil War re-enactment to another? Under them was a registration form, still to be filled out, for the convention of political items collectors at the Columbus Crown Plaza: July 31 to August 4. Guy had mentioned it, excited by the prospect of several ballrooms filled with political paraphernalia.

The old desk had an aura of mystery to it, like something from one of the Hardy Boys novels I'd loved in the fourth grade. By now the teenage heroes would have examined every nook and cranny. I came up with mostly empty drawers. Of course I felt for secret compartments, I'd gotten into the right mood. If any letters from Beecher Stowe were still here, it made sense that Guy would have concealed them. One drawer contained an envelope of postage stamps, a ledger of eBay sales, some fountain pens, Scotch tape, and a box of paper clips. You're an idiot, I laughed. This is what happens when you mix a little Freud with the Hardy Boys. Yet I felt disappointed, as if I'd failed Guy.

No letters, anyway. I piled up the papers, which Hedy might need later, and checked the drawers of the filing cabinet, all empty. Had Guy fallen here and struck his head against it? I tried to imagine Neil following Guy down to the basement and pushing him into the wall. He had a marriage – or divorce – to protect.

Or, out of jealousy, could Theo have shown up and threatened Guy?

If Neil was right, Theo had spied on them one night. Driven past the house, stalking.

My mind raced. In a minute I'd convince myself that Claire Warren had wrestled Guy for the Beecher Stowe letters.

Surely not Theo? He was afraid of his own shadow.

And Claire? Impossible. Not even for fifteen minutes of fame.

Though I'd never taken to Neil, he didn't seem like a rip-roaring psychopath.

Ray Hatchard, then? Or some previous hookup?

I'd wasted half an hour and, back upstairs, settled down to packing. Guy's books took no time, and his kitchenware only a little longer. The cupboard held four tall souvenir glasses. I turned one around in my hand, its red and yellow decal advertising "Aunt Fanny's Cabin's Mint Julep Smyrna, Georgia." The proprietor's image, a stereotypical Jemima, reminded drinkers of the dinner menu, which included "gen-u-wine" Smithfield ham. Did Guy bring the glasses home from a visit with his grandmother in Knoxville? He certainly wasn't mixing mint juleps. Perhaps Nick would want them.

Soon Guy's clothing filled several heavy-duty garbage bags in the living room. There was nothing here to shock Hedy or Nick: no pornographic DVDs, no box of flavored condoms, and no address book of unfamiliar names and telephone numbers, though that tube of KY, now disposed of, might have upset them. Guy, the beloved son, wasn't supposed to grow up.

Guy's Civil War collection demanded more care. I had no idea of the value of his objects, but they felt genuine, though they might deceive an untutored eye. One rusty belt buckle had been stamped CSA, for the Confederate States of America, and a broken scabbard read, simply, CS. I rolled them all in bubble wrap. Guy's photographs of the young soldiers saddened me most, since he'd taken his place with the dead, though for no grand cause. It seemed wrong that he'd had no funeral.

Don't go there now. I took the boxes into the living room and lined them along one wall, so that Hedy and Nick could avoid the rest of the house. Looking about, I realized that Hedy's sculptures remained on the mantel. She'd never explained what compelled her to repeat her wildlife subjects, but an artist makes things, maybe that's explanation enough. After wrapping the raccoons, I held the badger in hand. Its shape, its glazing, and the startled look on the creature's face made this piece one of Hedy's best. Later, she'd want it, she'd regret giving it away, so I put bubble wrap around it and set the sculpture with the raccoons.

About to take a final walk through the house, I heard someone knock on the front door. I hadn't mentioned the pack-up to Sheila, who might have spotted my car in Guy's yard and been curious. But Hedy stood at the door. "It didn't seem fair to leave it all to you," she said.

"Don't say that, I wasn't expecting you. We've known each other a hundred years."

She made an effort to smile.

"You haven't been sleeping," I said.

"Not very well." She came through the doorway, into the living room. Old bungalows like this one rarely have a hallway or foyer.

"You really didn't have to come, Hedy."

"Guy's with us all the time, but he's not with us any more. I can't say what I mean."

"Is Nick in the car? Is he alright?"

"He hasn't had any more chest pains, so I told him to rest at home." Hedy looked about at the boxes. "You're finished already?"

99

Probably out of habit she'd put on her bright lipstick, but no bangles or hair bow. She seemed gray, and aged, yet still beautiful.

"It didn't take that long. Wouldn't it have been good for Nick to get out?"

"He's very depressed, and that frightens me. It's almost like his last breakdown. There were days when he didn't get out of bed, he just lay there staring at the ceiling. Now he gets dressed and sits in the living room all day, blank."

"The last time…"

"He finally pulled out of it. After six months, and with some tranquillizers. I'm going to suggest them next week. I don't want to wait longer."

I leaned an arm against the mantel. "You look tired. Why don't you sit in the recliner."

"I can't stay still." Hedy paced about the room and then peered out the window.

"Did you hear from the police again?"

"Nothing more. They've called Guy's death 'undetermined,' that's it. I told you the coroner filed his report and the police did, too. They've signed off on Guy."

"They mustn't have any leads." I certainly wasn't going to mention Neil or Theo.

"I still think it was a home invasion. And it's killing us." She set her purse on one of the cardboard boxes.

"You're strong, Hedy, you have to count on that. It's awful, what you're both going through. I hate any talk about 'letting go' and 'closure'. It's too easy. It's cruel."

"Thanks." She smiled, her eyes shining, moist. "I don't know how we'll survive this."

"You've got to."

"I remember every minute of our marriage. Women can do that. We're not cold, like men. That's what drew me to Nick –

he wasn't a cold man. I'd never met anyone like him before. For the first time I didn't feel alone, and I knew with Nick I'd never have to be alone again. Things change in a marriage but not that. In a real marriage you're never alone again."

"It must have been hard for you, watching Guy without someone."

"He didn't have many friends – he kept to himself, he was like us. People liked him and he got along with everybody but he preferred his own company."

"No one special?"

"He mentioned a woman at work, at the clinic. I think he was interested. She was a few years older. Forty or so. And she has a daughter in high school."

"A dentist?"

"No, another technician. But she was Catholic. Very devout, he said. And with our beliefs that might have been difficult. I didn't encourage him. I think they'd gone out for pizza once or twice. He hadn't known her long."

"You never met the woman?"

"Oh, no."

Just new colleagues, of course. If only I'd found a diary or journal strategically hidden. The convenient deus ex machina. But not even an address book, nothing of the sort. Then it struck me that I hadn't come across Guy's cell phone, or his laptop.

"I didn't see his Beecher Stowe letters anywhere, and I practically took the desk apart."

"They might still be with one of the experts, to authenticate them."

"Or someone broke in and…" I suggested.

"We warned him not to talk about them."

"Do the police know about the letters?"

"I'm sure we told them."

"That's good. I've set aside a few things you might want. There was a collection of poems by Rumi on the night table. I saw the inscription from you and Nick."

"Oh, yes, I remember it. A birthday present. He was fourteen, I think."

"It didn't have a date."

"No, I wouldn't have put one." She shrugged.

Maybe the omission had something to do with her beliefs about eternal time.

"And some funny tall glasses. With decals from a restaurant in Georgia. Guy told me how much he liked visiting Nick's mother in Tennessee, and about their trips to old battle sites. She probably took him there on an outing."

"When did he say that?" she asked abruptly.

I'd forgotten the bad blood between the two women. "The night I dropped off the kettle."

Another shrug. "It could have been."

She didn't seem interested in the glasses, so I said, "The boxes with papers are heavy, I'll carry them out for you."

"Did you remember to take the badger?"

"You'll want it later," I said, gesturing toward the box that held it. "It's very fine, and Guy loved it. He told me so."

"You have to keep it, please. I insist. I'll never make another. I want you to have it. We go back a long time."

After I retrieved the badger, and put several boxes in the trunk of her car, Hedy drove off, but first she blew a kiss at me. Our old bond still held us.

13

Sheila's house, several blocks from Guy's, was surrounded by a
flower garden out of the pages of a horticulture magazine. She'd
missed her calling: landscape design. Along with the iris and
peonies, delphinium and bleeding-hearts, now blooming pro-
fusely, she'd mixed less common plants like penstemon and bap-
tisia and yarrow. And she made certain I knew their correct
names, because cuttings often made their way into my yard.

After parking in the drive I waved as Sheila came around
from the back of her house. Tonight I was going to re-record the
message on her answering machine. "Let's sit on the patio, it's
nice out. Would you drink a light beer? I'm counting calories
again." She wiped her hands on her jeans, went into the house,
and soon returned with two open bottles and her cigarettes. We
sat at a wooden picnic table on the flagstone patio she'd built for
herself.

"This time there was a bag of dog shit by my front door, so
I had the police out. I'm hoping for fingerprints on the bag.
Loretta's in the county system, it should be an easy search."

"If she was the one…"

"Who else, I'd like to know? I wanted to press charges but
there's no proof yet. I have some valuable things here, and if that
bitch gets in again there's gonna be hell to pay."

The tougher Sheila tried to sound, the sadder she seemed.
"You don't think it was Brad?"

"He's provoked me plenty. I still have some of his crap locked in the garage. Would you believe it, he has a fancy set of golf clubs?"

"Why don't you just give him his things?"

"He knows why." She lit a cigarette and inhaled as if her life depended on it. "He owes me money and I want it back. Twelve hundred bucks – that's a lot to me."

The beer didn't taste bad, just watery. "Did you tell the police about the money?"

"Sure. They said I should give Brad whatever belongs to him. You men stick together. If I could afford it I'd get a restraining order, but you probably need a lawyer." She took a long swig of beer, then rubbed her eyes with the back of her hand. "I don't want to talk about it."

Okay, I thought. "Last Saturday I packed up Guy's house for Nick and Hedy."

"You didn't tell me."

"I just wanted to get it over with."

"God, it's terrible. I miss him. Were your friends there?"

"No, I did it for them. I wish I'd known him better."

"What did you find?"

"His clothes, the standard housewares, that kind of stuff."

"And?" She missed him but was curious.

"His Civil War books and memorabilia. I don't know their value. That time I googled Confederate mementos…"

"What?"

"The night I took the kettle to Guy, he told me about some websites, and a few days later I looked at them. Some of the prices were pretty high. There was a sword with a broken handle going for five grand."

Her eyes widened. "I wonder if they'll sell his stuff. He was so proud of his collection. You should ask them to donate it to the library."

"I can't do that. They've just lost their son. It would be heart-less."

"Depends how you ask. What else did you find?"

"Guy hadn't lived there long enough to own very much."

"What about his laptop?" she ventured.

"It wasn't on his desk. I didn't find his cell phone either. And there was no land line."

"Nobody his age has one. I'll bet the police are checking out his cell. There hasn't been anything more in the papers."

"There's nothing to report. Hedy said the coroner called Guy's death 'undetermined.'"

"Undetermined?" Sheila lit another cigarette and took a lan-guorous drag. The tips of her fingers were starting to yellow from nicotine. I used to know a lot of people who smoked, and for a moment the scent took me back in time, not unpleas-antly.

"They have to call it something. It wasn't suicide, or a homi-cide."

"I wonder what's on Guy's computer? If the hard-drive wasn't damaged. You could ask your friends."

"Sheila, please, don't refer to them as 'your friends.' They have names."

"Sure. Okay." She glowered at me.

"Well, they do have names. What do you have against them?"

"I don't like them, isn't that enough? But for a starter, they drained the life out of Guy. I've known him a long time. Maybe you've known his parents longer, but I've known Guy."

"He was never around much," I said too defensively. I'd begun to regret ignoring Guy. I saw some of my own youthful confusion in him, along with his eagerness to please.

"He loved the mall. He'd worked there, remember?" She crushed her cigarette stub in a red glass ash tray, and it glowed. "When he got out of the army. Ten years ago. No, more."

"What did he do?" I wished I'd known more about Guy's stint in the army. He'd been overseas in Germany, and just missed being deployed in the Kosovo war; he must have learned something about himself.

"He was a floorwalker at the mall. He couldn't adjust to civilian life, he couldn't hold down a job. So his mother got him one there."

"Like those retired guys…"

"Exactly. It's not a job for a young man, keeping an eye out for shoplifters. But I guess there's no stress."

"After the army, probably not. Wasn't he bored?"

"He didn't seem to mind, and everyone liked him. That's when we got to know each other. Some days we'd have coffee if no one was around. He just couldn't decide what to do with himself, and that's not a crime." She looked at me accusingly.

"I didn't say it was."

"You people at the college…"

"Sheila, let's not talk about 'you people.' It's hard enough to make any sense of what happened to Guy."

If I expected Sheila to back down it would be a long wait. I took another mouthful of flat beer, she flicked her lighter a couple of times, and then asked, "You think there's something suspicious about his accident?"

"I didn't at first. But old people fall, and sick people, not healthy young men. And now that I've been down in his basement a few times, I can't understand it."

"What do Nick and Hedy say?"

"They don't have any answers."

"I hope you noticed I used their names," she added.

I had to laugh.

"Guy was an only child, and you know what that's like," she said. "You and me and Guy, we understand. Everybody thinks we're spoiled, that we got all the attention, all the goodies, but there's such a thing as too much attention. And when your parents get old, you have all the responsibility. You looked after your parents, you know what I'm talking about."

"You can say that again. But there are advantages too."

"I love my mother but sometimes I can't breathe."

"Guy loved his parents, I'm sure of it."

"I could tell you things," she said.

"What do you mean?"

"Things," she repeated.

"Don't be coy, Sheila."

"You really want to hear? Just don't blame me, I've warned you."

"I'm not blaming anyone."

"Okay, then. For starters, Guy was molested."

"You're sure of that? I've never heard about it. How do you know?"

"He told me himself – that's how. It's one reason he's been seeing a shrink." She paused for a moment. "And his shrink told him to stop concealing it."

"It's terrible, I had no idea. Who was it?" I nearly looked away. "When did it happen?"

"You're not gonna like it." She sat back in her chair. Though her tone of voice suggested caution, she had a self-satisfied look.

"C'mon, Sheila, don't tease."

"Your buddy. Nick. His father."

It was like she'd tossed a hand grenade to me. "That's impossible!"

"I don't think so. Not according to Guy." She paused again, for effect. "Nope, not at all."

"You must have it wrong. I can't believe it."

"Well, Guy's shrink did. And he wanted Guy to keep a memory journal. You didn't find one, did you?"

"Nothing like that. A lot of papers on his desk, but no journal."

"I don't know if he'd started one, but we talked about it. I thought it was a good idea."

"When was this supposed to have happened?"

"Years ago. Guy was twelve or so and Nick took him on a camping trip. They'd never gone on one before – it was very exciting – and the first night it turned out they had only one sleeping bag. They'd forgotten the second one at home."

"What does that prove? This is crazy."

"See, I warned you. You want details?"

"Just tell me, okay?"

"They were curled up against each other, practically in each other's arms, and Guy got a hard-on. You know what teenage boys are like, they walk around with permanent hard-ons. Then Nick said there was nothing wrong with it, that it was perfectly normal, and as he brushed against him Guy came right away, he didn't know what was happening, it had never happened before. And next thing, he felt his father's hard-on pressed against his side, and when he touched it, well, you can guess the rest. He was desperate to please his father, that's all he wanted, Nick's approval. It was pitch black in their tent, he couldn't see a thing, and outside the woods were so still, he said, it felt like they were the last people on earth. He remembered not sleeping, just leaning against his father's body to keep warm, certain in the morning Nick would be angry at him, though he didn't know why. And that night always stayed with him, even when he tried to forget it."

"He said he was ashamed?"

"No, not ashamed. It's odd, but he said it was like they had one body, they weren't separate people, yet at the same time he knew nothing would be the same again. He cried while he told me."

"And then?"

"There's not much more. But the trouble was, Guy trusted in his father, he adored him. Isn't that enough? Nick told Guy not to talk about it again, it had to be their secret. But Guy didn't understand why. He couldn't imagine his father would do anything wrong. The next day they cut their camping short. Then on the way home Nick said what they did was okay the one time but that they mustn't do it again, or even talk about it. Oh, and this part's a killer: it might spoil Guy for marriage. That's what he told his son. And Guy was shipped off to his grandmother for the rest of the summer."

"Does Hedy know?"

"Guy never told her, but he wondered if she knew, if his parents had discussed it. But he was afraid to ask. He wanted to but Nick kept putting him off, because they weren't supposed to talk about it. So he blamed himself."

"I suppose Nick was afraid of him, if any of this is true, but…"

"He deserved it, the bastard. Then the newspapers started to fill up with stories about all those priests molesting boys, you know how it went on and on, and after a while Guy got the picture – his wonderful father had molested him."

"It doesn't make any sense, Sheila. Usually things like that happen more than once."

"One time's enough, don't you think?"

"If that's really what happened, it almost sounds like a couple of kids fooling around, you know, two boys masturbating together…"

"Only one of the boys was a grown man," Sheila cut me off. "And his father."

"You're sure this wasn't a fantasy? Something his shrink suggested? There are books about repressed memory and false memory, it's a dangerous thing."

"Well, have it your way. I believed Guy."

"He was having an affair," I said, deciding to tell her about Neil Breuler.

"I know that. He told me. That guy who rents from Theo."

"You've known all along?"

"Sure. I didn't realize you knew too."

"The police questioned him but nothing came of it. He might have been one of the last people to see Guy alive."

"Do your friends know about him?"

They were 'your friends' again, but I wouldn't object. "I don't think so. Hedy said that Guy was interested in a woman at work, another dental technician. She wanted him to be happy."

Sheila shook her head. "They're idiots, truly. And don't try to excuse Nick, don't call it a mistake."

"I'd never say that. I can't imagine what he was thinking. This is impossible."

"He wasn't thinking, obviously." Sheila nearly laughed. "To leave Guy hanging, as if nothing had happened, that was mean. Remember what it's like to be twelve. Imagine how that felt. It's no wonder he joined the army as soon as he could."

I thought of Neil's story about the army officer who'd hit on Guy. "But he came back to his family."

"Where else would he go? Abused women return to their husbands, that's not news. Guy's all torn up inside. I mean he was. I still can't believe he's dead."

"How long have you known this?"

"Months and months. He told me in February. On Valentine's Day. I was supposed to see Brad that night but he never showed up, so when Guy called I invited him over, I was pretty upset and one thing led to another, we got talking, and when I asked about his therapy it all came out. I told him to confront his father but he wouldn't hear of it, he blamed himself for everything. He even said that Nick had probably forgotten it. I'm only telling you now because Guy's dead. He made me promise not to say a word."

"And there's nothing we can do."

"That's up to you."

"How? If I said anything Nick would only deny it. And it would destroy Hedy."

"So Nick wins." She tipped out the last cigarette from its package.

"But his son's dead. That's a terrible punishment."

"It's not bad enough," Sheila said. "Not by a long shot."

14

Quid nunc? as they say. What now? Aristotle would have probably thrown up his hands.

A week had passed since Sheila's bombshell. I hadn't heard from Nick or Hedy, and if they didn't want to talk to me, I would respect their wishes. Anyway, I didn't want to talk to them just yet. They were bereft, and I had no idea what I might say.

Glad to be busy at work, I'd just gotten back to my office from a budget meeting when the telephone rang. Of all people it was Daphne Eliades, who wanted to meet for lunch. She was in town for the Memorial Day weekend, staying with an old friend, not her brother. That fact alone should have warned me. She chose the local inn, which has a captive audience in this one-hotel town. Some sprucing-up was overdue but that didn't stop its regulars.

We met in the inn's lobby, a short walk from the library, and cheek kissed. "Theo used to like lunching here," I said, without adding, "When he was still willing to leave the house."

As we crossed the restaurant, I spotted Claire Warren holding court at a table for six. She caught my eye and waved.

"Are you still enjoying life in Bay Village?" I asked Daphne, before picking up a menu that promised "traditional Midwest cooking" like quesadillas.

Daphne ignored her menu. "I don't know where to begin." She had dressed for a special occasion in a silky black shirtwaist printed with small white geometric designs, and as usual wore a lot of gold. "This is in confidence. You promise? It's about Theo. I'm very worried."

So she'd also been alarmed by his prolonged moodiness.

"Ever since Neil moved in, Theo's not been himself. We always spend Greek Easter together, it's the highpoint of the Orthodox year. All the holy week services…"

"Yes, he invited me once."

"Then you know it's not always the same date as your Easter."

"I don't celebrate holidays any more."

"It's our tradition." She stopped for a moment, took a drink of water, and then continued. "Last month I expected Theo to come. I've found a lovely church and even joined Philoptohos, that's the Hellenic Ladies' Society. Anyway, he wasn't sick…"

"I can't get him to go for a pizza, Bay Village must seem too far. And he hates highway driving, day or night."

She opened her menu, glanced down at it, frowned, and reached for her purse.

"What's wrong, Daphne?"

She unclasped the purse, took out a tube of lipstick and spread a thin layer of glossy pink over her mouth. Without a mirror, she touched the edge of her lips, where the upper one met the lower, with her right index finger, smudging the lipstick. "It's like this," she said, starting over. "Theo's supposed to move near me, you know that. What you don't know – what he doesn't know – is that I'm getting married."

"That's great, though you don't look very happy about it."

She frowned once more. "But I am, I am. He's a wonderful man, I'd like you to meet him. It's just complicated." She looked down at her purse again, as if she couldn't find a way to continue.

The word *complicated* is usually an excuse for behaving badly. "We should order," I suggested. "I have to be back at work in an hour."

"Oh, yes, sorry."

I motioned to a waitress. "Why haven't you told Theo?"

"He pretends everything's fine, but it isn't. I've looked out for him as long as I can remember. Fortunately my husband never minded. If we'd had children it might have been different."

"I'm sure Theo appreciated it."

"I did my best to make him happy. When I had dinner guests, Theo was always invited. I suggested movies and…" She paused, looking about the dining room. "He's my only family."

"That's what he says about you."

"Things will be different now. My fiancé, Stavro – I met him at church – he's more old-fashioned. He was born in Crete. He's a wonderful guy, a widower, and I'm lucky. But he spends half the year in Florida. In Tarpon Springs. There's a large Greek community and Stavro has a house with several acres. He's had it for ten years, since his wife died…"

"That sounds very nice. The house, I mean."

"It is. But he usually goes there from the beginning of December to the end of April."

"Theo could visit. Theoretically, at least."

She smiled for the first time.

"You can't live your life for your brother."

Her smile disappeared. "My late husband said that. Not often, but he would have agreed. And he liked him, I know he did."

"Maybe Stavro will, too. You need to talk to Theo."

I expected Daphne to bring up Neil again but she never mentioned him, and we finished our lunch while I tried not to look at my watch. Perhaps she was satisfied.

Back at the library I telephoned Sheila, not expecting to find her at home, only to leave a message. Could we meet later? I offered to bring some Chinese take-out. Instead, she told me to drop by around nine, she had gardening to do. "After supper's the only time I have for my own garden," she added.

Sheila had no reason to make up stories about Guy and Nick. I'd gone over our last conversation so many times it now buzzed around in my head with the persistence of early summer flies. My questions weren't about disbelief, yet disbelief lingered, and egotism too: how could I have missed Guy's dilemma? Perhaps I'd never gotten close to him because I sensed that any interest shown in Guy might make Hedy and Nick uncomfortable.

Once more I parked in Sheila's driveway, but she wasn't in sight so I looked about. Her house was on the wrong side of South Main, down past the police department. Unlike Guy's rental, it had been built before 1900. One of the older homes around, the two-storey wooden affair was painted gray, with white gingerbread recalling the previous century. A rap on the front door brought her from the back of the house. "You're late," she said. "Watch it, don't let the cats out."

"It's only ten after," I said, carefully opening the door.

Last year Sheila had taken in two black strays, given them names and struggled to tame them. She now fed a family of feral cats that lived on her block, claiming half a dozen regulars.

"I put on some coffee," she replied, as I entered the living room. Both cats fled to their hiding places. "Happy's the friendly one," she said.

While Sheila and Hedy were drawn to antiques they could not afford, Sheila became attached to her best finds. "I'm keeping them as old-age insurance," she'd explained more than once. Anything Victorian caught their attention, though Hedy coveted the less ornate objects. More antique dolls filled a glass case in Sheila's dining room, which may be why she ate in the kitchen: you wanted to get away from all the beady glass eyes in those porcelain heads.

The kitchen had a retro look, like something preserved from a fifties' sitcom, or set up to resemble one. As soon as we sat at the table, Sheila lit a cigarette and said, "Well?"

"I keep wondering if Hedy knew about Guy."

"She probably didn't want to."

"Her son's suffering and she doesn't notice, it's hard to believe."

"Foul things, I smoke too much." Sheila watched the cigarette burn between her fingers.

"Do you really think he was telling you the truth?"

"How can I know? But why would he lie? I figured you'd start to defend them…"

"That's not fair, Sheila. I'm not defending anyone. But it seems odd, that's all. You'd think Nick would have tried it again. A 'repeat offender' – isn't that the term? Guy might not have told you everything. He could've been testing you, to see how you'd react. Or maybe he'd blocked out…"

"Kids are abused all the time. It's probably happening to someone around the corner right now. When I was fourteen I used to babysit for this la-di-da professor, and when he'd drive me home he'd put his hand on the back of my neck, just so." She caressed the spot with her left hand. "And he'd ask if I was tired. I knew what the bastard had in mind when he looked down at my boobs, he was working up the nerve to try something. Finally I told his dumb wife that I was too busy to sit for them. Believe me, women know what men think about."

"Not all men."

"Bullshit. When I told my mother about it she remembered how a family friend had touched her breasts when she was twelve, they were at an amusement park, on the Ferris wheel, for

God's sake . He had a daughter the same age as Mother but that didn't stop him from copping a feel. I'll bet Guy thought no one would believe him."

"I'm just not sure this adds up. You'd think it would have happened more than once, and, I don't know, it sounded like Guy was attracted to his father – something out of Freud."

"Screw Freud, I wasn't there. And I've never been a teenage boy. My old man sure didn't turn me on but he had a cute younger brother. Dead now from the booze, but he was cute back then. I loved it when we played badminton and he took his shirt off."

She lost me, and I tried to remember Guy as a teenager. A gawky quiet kid, often with his nose in a sci-fi book, or out in the woods behind their house. Didn't Hedy once say he'd been teased at school because of their diet and the lunches she packed for him? Maybe bullied, too. And then, after a campout with his father, he'd seen how his body worked, and felt more isolated than before.

"No wonder Guy always seemed withdrawn. I wish he could have told someone sooner."

"Who, for instance? I'd love to hear Lady Hedda's reaction. That ought to be something," she chuckled.

"I'm sure she didn't know…"

"That's what you want to think," Sheila interrupted.

"She does believe some pretty odd things. Not just all her past-lives stuff, we don't need to go there, though she's big on 'soul history' – that's what she calls it."

"No shit." She stubbed out the cigarette butt and pushed the pack away from herself. "There could be something to karma, you know. I must have been a real ball-breaker in my last life, and I'm paying for it now."

"That time the police came to the mall, after Guy died, did you talk with them?"

"I said I hadn't seen Guy, he hadn't called me. That's all."

"Why didn't you tell them about Nick? You believed Guy."

"The cops are idiots. What good have they ever done me? They probably would've thought I was making it up, and Guy wasn't around to defend himself."

We weren't getting anywhere like this. "Tell me more about Guy's neighbors, the ones…"

"There's not much to tell. They have an old boxer that wakes them several times during the night to go out to pee, and they noticed the light was still on in Guy's basement. I don't know what time it was."

"Who notices things like that?"

"Well, they did. You can only watch a dog pee for so long. What are you getting at?"

"Nothing adds up, that's all. Guy's dead, and Neil Breuler was his boyfriend, or something like that, and you tell me Guy was abused by his father…"

"I should've kept my mouth shut."

"I'm glad you told me. But it changes everything."

"How?"

Sheila wouldn't want to hear about my friendship puzzles, or Aristotle. And while I still wondered if Guy's accusation was the work of an over-eager therapist, she wouldn't have listened to doubt.

"Do you figure Nick's really gay?" she asked.

"No, that's not what this is about. I just can't make any sense of it."

"Well, a lot of married men swing both ways, and if they cheat on their wives it's probably easier with a guy who won't make demands, or want to settle down. Any warm hole will do."

"I wouldn't put it quite that way, Sheila. You never mince words."

"At least I don't bother with married men anymore, I'm immune. But your friends, I told you, they're idiots."

When I didn't reply at once, she said, "I forgot about the coffee. Want some now?" In the same breath she stood up, filled two mugs and brought them to the table, which was covered by a faded cloth embroidered with cherries.

"Neil came to see me, in my office," I said, reaching for a mug.

"What for?"

"He knows that Guy's parents are old friends of mine, and I think he was curious if they'd heard about him. From Guy or the police. He's in the middle of a divorce."

"Guy wouldn't have talked about him," Sheila observed. "What does Theo say?"

"I didn't tell him that Neil dropped by."

Sheila nodded. "Some day Theo's going to stop being depressed and he'll start to scream and never stop. They'll have to cart him off screaming."

"He's not that bad." I wouldn't mention Neil's hunch that Theo had once followed him to Guy's place.

"If you say so." She dismissed my comment with a wave of hand.

"But today Daphne Eliades invited me to lunch. She's getting married again."

"Does he have money?"

"Maybe she likes the guy, I didn't ask. He has houses in Bay Village and Florida."

"That's what I need, someone well-off." She shook her head in mock despair.

"She's worried about how Theo will take it."

Laughing, Sheila reached for her cigarettes, touched the pack and then pushed it away. "You mean she doesn't want him to move in with them? But he's selling his house, isn't he?"

"That's the problem."

"We've all got our problems. You haven't asked about Brad."

"Has something happened?"

"I don't want to talk about it."

"You always say that, Sheila."

We stared at each other for a few seconds.

"Alright then," she said. "They couldn't find a fingerprint match with Loretta, but that doesn't mean she didn't leave the crap. And she's still waking me in the middle of the night, so I unplug my phone. I told Mother to call my cell if there's an emergency. The cops can't do a thing without evidence, and probably don't want to spend the time or money. I'm small fry, remember. If someone was phoning the president of the college in the middle of the night, they'd know who it was. And I'm scared. The idea that someone hates me so much, so much they'll stay up all hours…"

"Have you heard from Brad?"

"I'm thinking of selling his golf clubs. They have to be worth something."

"Did you tell him that?"

"We haven't talked in a week. I've got to admit it's over, but I can't."

"You will, Sheila. Just give it time. You're a strong person – look how you take care of yourself." I refrained from adding, "You're better off without him."

"You don't know what it's like," she said. "I'm still in love."

She was locked in a bad torch song, but again I kept my tongue. I was past torch songs.

"That's the heart of it," she said with a sigh.

15

I woke at five and couldn't sleep again. Last night Hedy phoned and we planned to meet for lunch. Apprehensive, I wasn't ready to see them. Sheila's account of Guy's confession had left me at a loss. I wanted to confront Nick, yet it would mean the end of our friendship. Maybe there's a little cop in all of us, an accuser, and I'd rather be detached.

Now that Guy had been dead for six weeks, Hedy hoped to draw Nick out of himself. To start, there was a promising estate sale in Oberlin, and she insisted that he come along with her. Afterward we'd meet at a restaurant they liked. She also asked me to hand over Guy's keys to his landlady so that they wouldn't have to see the house again. A small request, I'd arranged to meet her there at ten o'clock, and was glad for one last go at Guy's place.

It was a clear bright morning, already too warm for May. In this part of the state people used to caution against putting in tomato plants before Memorial Day, because of late frost. Not this year. My garden looked tired, it couldn't stand the relentless ninety-plus heat. Before heading to Guy's I felt my pocket for his keys. Once again I didn't know what I was looking for.

Fortunately Helen Wheeler hadn't yet arrived and I had time to walk through the house by myself. I checked the closets, cupboards, even the drawers in the kitchen, and all were empty, as I'd left them. A broom with a yellow plastic handle rested against the bathroom door, so she must have been by. Goodwill had picked up Guy's furniture, and he might never have lived here. The only proof remained in the police photographs taken before they removed his body.

Back in the living room I tried to imagine what Guy might have felt when he moved into the house. I recalled my own first apartment and the sense of euphoria that accompanied it. I was angry for Guy. Only a month ago he would have begun his day here, made his plans, dreamed about the future. He hadn't fallen down in the basement, I was certain of that. He'd been arguing, he'd been pushed; someone had been with him. Even the police called his death "undetermined".

I heard footsteps on the porch stairs and went to the front door, where a woman in her seventies, with cropped gray hair, stood waiting. "Mrs. Wheeler?" I asked.

"That's me." She carried a pail in one hand and a large plastic bag in the other.

I explained again that I was a friend of Guy's parents.

"I remember," she said. "I've still got a good memory."

Her no-nonsense manner suggested a short fuse. "Sorry, I didn't mean…"

"Yes, you did, but that's okay. I'm used to it."

This was an opportunity I didn't want to miss. "Did you know Guy well?"

"I don't get to know my tenants, I mind my own business as long as they pay their rent on time. He seemed nice enough." She set down the pail and the plastic bag. "I've never found a dead body before. It's frightening, you know. He's my first dead tenant. You can't forget something like that. You think you've seen everything but it's not true. I certainly didn't like finding those bullets on his shelves."

"They were Civil War bullets," I said, as if that might make a difference.

"Bullets are bullets."

"I believe you're friends with Doris Carney. Her daughter, Sheila, does my gardening."

"We're in a bridge group together. We're the best players."

Here was my opening. "And your other tenants? The ones across the street…"

"You heard about them? They look out for me. When I rent to someone I don't want anyone else moving in without my permission. The water bill goes up…"

"I hadn't thought of that." Our voices seemed to echo in the empty living room. "Is there anything I should tell my friends? What about Guy's security deposit?"

"I'm keeping that. I had a lease with him and…"

"But he didn't break it, he died."

"All the same, I have to find new tenants. It's hard to rent a place where someone has died, I have to advertise all over again. And what about his car? It's still in the garage."

No one, in fact, had remembered Guy's car. And his bicycle must be there as well.

"He's paid up to the end of the month," she added brusquely. "You've got till then."

Five more days. Plenty of time to move the car. I finished my Saturday errands, trying not to think about Guy. Nick and Hedy had already taken a corner table at Aladdin's when I got to the restaurant. Their window overlooked the common where they'd first met, and, more than three decades later, might have seen their son plead with a boyfriend not to drop him. "Am I late?"

"We just got here ourselves," she said.

There was something about Hedy's face that seemed, well, noble. Not just refined or classic, but noble. Nick had an aspect of this as well, but in a lesser degree. It was always a pleasure to look at them, and I suspect they'd enjoyed my admiration and no longer felt it. Today her face had more color than the last time we met, and her hair seemed several shades darker, as if recently dyed. She wore a navy cotton pullover with a silver broach in the shape of a floral wreath pinned several inches below the neckline, not strictly mourning clothes yet sedate. She had, however, put on the turquoise eye shadow that Nick liked. She was hell bent on normalcy, and ordinarily I would have considered it touching.

"You look great," I said, pulling back a chair. "And you too, Nick. How are you feeling?"

"I'm better now. Thanks to Hedy." He reached for her hand.

His olive complexion still had a grayish tinge. "No more chest pains?"

"Not a one."

"He's recovered completely," Hedy said, her voice full of pride. "Like I knew he would. Even the doctors are impressed."

I had to watch myself. It wasn't possible to look at Nick without Sheila's words echoing in my mind. *Spoil him for marriage* had taken on a life of its own.

"I've been anticipating this all morning," Hedy said, without opening her menu. For the first time since Guy's death the copper healing bracelets were back on her wrists, though she didn't mention being in pain. Aladdin's was one of the few places in town where my friends could find a vegetarian meal that suited them, and they knew the menu by heart.

"Was it a good sale?" I asked.

"Nothing special," she said brightly.

"But it's been a good morning," Nick agreed. "Though I couldn't put a flag out for Memorial Day, I'm too upset about what's happening to my country. The Constitution means nothing to most people."

Guy had died, he'd been in the army, yet that wasn't reason enough for flag waving.

"Now we've heard…" he continued.

I sat back and listened to a convoluted lament about the media's slavish attention to Queen Elizabeth's Diamond Jubilee. After all, she belonged to a powerful group of investors who, along with the United Nations, were working to undermine America's global influence; there may even have been a connection to 9/11. How far can an overwrought imagination go? Though I hated the widening chasm between us, their conspiracy theories took more patience than I had. At times I'd wondered what Nick and Hedy would come up with next, but today it no longer mattered. "Where did you hear all of this?" I asked. "It's not in any newspaper I read."

"Of course not," Hedy said defiantly.

"Then where did you read otherwise?"

"I've told you before, I don't have to name my sources."

"We have our sources, too," Nick said, in duet.

The Antons were my friends and I didn't want to dismiss them as crackpots. Again, it seemed they needed to bait me, as if my resistance somehow proved them orphans in the storm. I nearly asked if they were as pleased with themselves as they appeared. Yet I wouldn't let go of our friendship, and this was my own fault, my problem – and really foolish at my age.

"Let's talk about something else," I suggested. "It's difficult when we have different facts. I know I've said that before."

"A lot of people think the way we do," Nick replied. "You'll see, this fall. I can't wait for the election."

"It's like a plague of despair," I said. "All this fear and anger."

Half of the country hated the sitting president, and the other half loathed his rival.

"We want our country back," Nick said softly.

"I know that, but finding meaning in life is trickier than politics…"

"We're not searching for the meaning of life," Hedy replied. "Not with our values. We already know what matters."

For a few minutes we ate in an awkward silence, their expressions indicating that I'd gone too far, I'd dared to object, to challenge them.

"This morning I gave the house keys to Mrs. Wheeler," I told them, hoping to change the subject for good. "And it occurred to me that I never saw Guy's computer or his cell phone when I packed up his place. But the night he'd shown me around they were there, I remember his cell phone on the kitchen table. Did the police take them?"

"Yes," Hedy said coolly. "They dropped them off last week."

"Then there was nothing useful on them…"

"Useful?" asked Nick.

"A lead about the people Guy knew…"

"We told them everything," Hedy said. "They even wanted to contact Guy's doctor, but he didn't have one – he was never sick, he used ours if he needed one."

"Did you ever hear of someone named Neil Breuler?"

Both looked at me cautiously but appeared unfamiliar with the name.

"Neil Breuler," I repeated.

"Who is he?" Hedy asked tentatively.

"He works at the college, in security. He knew Guy. I saw them together on the common a couple nights before Guy died. It was starting to rain and Guy was on his bike." I thought to add that they'd appeared to be arguing but didn't want to press my luck.

Hedy shook her head. "Guy never mentioned him."

"He was making new friends," I suggested quickly. "You have to do that in a new town."

Nick nodded. "Guy had been saving up for his own place. He was so excited about it."

"Have you heard from the woman he was dating?"

"No," Hedy said. "We didn't expect to."

I wondered if Guy had made her up, a cover to deflect their curiosity – another thing I wouldn't say. And I certainly couldn't ask if Nick had molested his son, not here, casually, over a plate of hummus: "Would you please pass the pita, and by the way, did you abuse Guy?" I could hardly ask that.

"I don't even remember her name," Hedy said. "And I don't want to think about it. Let's just enjoy our lunch. It's been a long time since I've had an appetite."

Nick had turned towards the window, a vacant expression on his face. Should I remind them that Guy's car and bike were still in his rented garage?

"We love the fried eggplant here," Hedy said.

Of course it had never occurred to me to search the trunk of Guy's car, or the glove compartment, but I assumed the police had been more thorough.

16

"So you didn't learn anything new?" Sheila asked. "You should have tried harder."

We were on our knees in my backyard, digging holes along the fence.

"In a restaurant, for God's sake? You've been to Aladdin's, I couldn't very well…"

"I would have. Poor Guy. You're sure no Nick Charles."

"Who?"

"The *Thin Man* detective, you know. But then I'm not like his wife, either. We're just a menopausal mess and a gay geezer."

"C'mon, Sheila, don't talk like that. And maybe there's nothing more, that's always possible."

With a mock frown she tossed a trowelful of soil into the hole I was digging.

Sheila had brought over three pots of plants, fall anemones, which I'd once admired in her garden. They weren't gifts, she charged five bucks a pot, but she had to make a living.

"These are a bitch to dig up, the root system really spreads. I think two are lavender and the other one's white. And they grow pretty fast."

"My kind of plant."

"If you want more I'll bring them next week. This afternoon I'm getting Mother, we're gonna barbecue."

"Theo's coming by later for drinks."

"I still can't believe Daphne's getting married." Sheila used her trowel to point to the hole I was digging, and said, "That's not deep enough."

"Well, she's not married yet. A lot can happen before a wedding."

She laughed heartily. "This is no holiday for me. I have another yard to check on, and it's gonna be a scorcher."

We sprinkled fresh topsoil into the holes, settled the plants in place, and then mounded more soil around them. "There," Sheila said, patting the ground. "Remember to water these again tonight. But don't drown them. Sometimes you drown things."

Sheila liked to have the last word.

"They'll drink this up now," she said, reaching for a watering can and gently tipping its spout to control the water's flow.

"Looking good," I said.

She nodded agreement. "I can sit for a minute, it's only ten o'clock."

We moved to the back steps and surveyed the garden.

"Aren't you smoking?" I asked.

"I'm trying to give it up again."

"Good for you."

"Don't be smug just because you're not tempted."

"Are you still getting those phone calls?"

"She missed a couple nights and it unnerved me."

"Maybe she got bored." Now I was saying "she" too. "Have you tried to reach Brad?"

Sheila looked away sheepishly, and then shook her head. "He spent the night. Last Saturday. I'm a fool, don't say it. A goddam fool."

"You're getting back together?"

"Oh no, I don't think so. He doesn't want that. It was one of those fucks for old times' sake. I can't get him out of my system, that's all."

"Is he still with Loretta?"

"I didn't ask. What's the point? But he wanted his golf clubs. Maybe that's what it was all about. A little sick exchange."

"And you gave them to him?"

"Yeah, what the hell. I couldn't bring up the money, I just couldn't. Now I hate myself for it."

"Sometimes…"

"Don't make excuses for me. I'm a big girl. But I'm also a fool. You're lucky you don't want anyone. It's terrible, wanting someone."

"We've all been there, once or twice."

"At least," she corrected with a rueful snicker. "I'm so tired of my problems, I'd like to run away but I don't know where, and anyway I can't afford to." She wiped her forehead with the back of her hand. "Just don't say anything, okay?"

We sat looking at the yard, sun beating down on the lawn, a square of burning green.

"Remember to water those plants," Sheila said finally, moving on to her next job.

After she'd gone I worked on my conference paper. When your family's dead, and the people you've cared most for are also gone, there's a heavy glum air to Memorial Day. I wasn't much interested in conferences but the college liked them and picked up the tab. By the time Theo arrived I was satisfied with a few pages and ready for a break.

"I thought you'd bring Neil along," I said when he stood at my front door.

"He's away for the weekend. But Daphne's in town, she's staying with me."

She must have changed her plans.

"There's something I want to tell you. Daph already knows," Theo said, settling in a corner of the sofa. "Neil's moving out."

I sat at the opposite end. "Aren't you getting along?"

"We haven't argued. He's going back to his wife. He said maybe they could sort things out. And he misses his daughters."

Did Neil think he could sidestep the police by moving down Highway 58 to another small town? "I'm surprised his wife will have him back."

Theo had a sour expression on his face. "That's where he is now. With his family. He called it a trial run, but it's not going to work."

"Your Greek sixth sense," I teased.

"I'm serious," he said. "It's too late for them. His oldest daughter graduates from high school next year, and the youngest a year later. After that his wife won't want him, you'll see."

"He's not an answer for you, Theo. You've got too much time on your hands. You don't need Neil."

"What should I do with my time? Volunteer work?"

"Forget Neil for a start." There are days when it seems that my friends want to drive me crazy. "Are you up for the first gin and tonic of the summer?"

"I'd rather have some wine."

"Okay, wine it is. Want to sit on the back porch? Sheila was here this morning and the garden looks great."

"It's an oven out there. You know I can't take hot weather."

Theo was going to hate Florida. But for someone who disliked heat, he made few concessions to it, and wore one of his starched Oxford-cloth shirts – always blue and white striped – with the sleeves rolled up to his elbows. Looking shell-shocked, he followed me into the kitchen while I made my drink and poured his wine, and we went back into the living room without saying a word.

"How long has Neil been planning this move?"

Theo took several swallows of wine. "He told me just before he left for the weekend."

"Being questioned about Guy must have scared him. The police would scare anyone."

He winced. "I never know when they're going to show up."

"Well, they aren't shadowing you."

"You certainly don't think Neil had anything to do with that death? Just because you saw them together one night…"

"I don't understand why the police took him to the station. Wouldn't anyone be more relaxed in their home, and open up?"

"Neil was pretty uptight when the police came. I knew he hadn't done anything wrong but he acted odd, and they picked up on it."

"How can you be so sure…"

"I don't follow him around, if that's what you mean. You don't think I follow him around?" He smiled awkwardly.

"I didn't say that."

"Neil wouldn't hurt anyone. Last month a bird got into the basement and he was so gentle with it. I hate things flying near me, it would still be down there today but Neil took over, he's like that. He has a kind heart."

Theo concealed his distress better than Sheila did, but he wasn't convincing himself.

"Did you know he came to see me at the library?" Given Theo's news, I didn't mind admitting it now.

He looked straight at me, suspiciously. "No. Why?"

"He wanted to know if the Antons had heard about him from Guy, but they hadn't. They still believe Guy had a girlfriend."

"Did you tell Sheila about him and Guy?"

"She already knew. Guy told her a while ago."

Theo shook his head. "He needs to watch out."

"What for? I saw Hedy and Nick the other day and when I brought up Neil's name they looked blank. What are you protecting him from?"

"I'm not protecting him," he said with great effort.

"Well, that's what it sounds like. Don't be angry, I'm on your side." I nursed my G&T without much pleasure, the fizz gone flat.

"Did he say anything about me?"

"That you worry too much, that's all. Probably I shouldn't have told you, but his mind's on other things."

"He hasn't called all weekend and it's a holiday."

"Give it a rest, Theo, okay?"

"I know about your lunch with Daphne," he said, a hint of accusation in his voice. "She doesn't like him either."

"Then you should listen to her. You've got too much free time, you're too smart to do nothing."

"Work is your answer for everything."

"There's nothing wrong with caring about your work."

He hesitated for a moment. "Not if you're hiding in it."

"Is that what you think I'm doing?"

"Well, it's not my answer. I never liked working. Most people don't. And Daphne's getting married, that changes..." He stopped, sighing.

"But you don't live together. Anyway, this isn't the nineteenth century, when families shared a big house forever."

"I would've liked the nineteenth century."

"Maybe you'll like Stavro. Don't write him off yet."

The sun had come around to the front of the house and light filled the living room – it almost poured through the windows onto us – sharpening Theo's every expression, each infinitesimal grimace.

"You can't possibly understand about twins," he said. "I've read all the studies, every one of them," he added emphatically. "There's a connection between twins that other siblings don't have. I can't explain it. And it's not that I'm jealous, but I feel like my life's over. There's no point in selling my house now, no point in moving. Maybe it was a bad idea from the start, but everyone doesn't want to be alone. I'm a nervous type, Chief. Next thing, you'll be telling me to get a dog."

I had to laugh. "There are worse options."

"Some awful little poodle I can carry around with me like one of those dowagers, is that your plan for me?"

We were both laughing now.

"But it has to have a rhinestone collar," I said. "I'll buy it for you."

"For little Fifi, you mean."

"As long as I'm her favorite uncle."

"Oh, you'll be her uncle," Theo said. "You can count on it."

17

My throat constricted as I opened the morning paper at my desk in the library. I began reading, but *The Chronicle*'s headline already told the story: "Antiques Dealer Shot." My first instinct was to telephone Sheila. Trouble trips you up like that.

After managing to crawl to her front porch, the wounded middle-aged woman had been found last night by neighbors, shortly before ten o'clock. Identified as Sheila Carney – "a well-known Oberlin antiques dealer, who had a booth at the mall" – she was in critical condition. With a full investigation underway, the police would welcome any leads, any reportings of suspicious people in the area. A dark grainy photograph of Sheila looked out at me, a photo from a happier moment, never intended for an article like this.

Where was Sheila now? Anxious to speak with her, I stared down at a newspaper that offered little help. "A struggle had apparently taken place" – the bland words, so calm and contained, were an affront. Day after day we're told that no home is safe, any moment we might be part of CNN's "Breaking News." Yet why would someone harm Sheila? What possible motive? The police certainly knew about Brad and Loretta, Sheila had reported them often enough, although nothing came of her complaints. After I'd re-recorded her phone message, she continued to receive the middle-of-the-night calls, so before bed she unplugged her phone from its wall jack.

I'd met Brad only once, when he accompanied Sheila to help carry away an old chest of drawers of mine, and wasn't sure if I would recognize him. Could he have been that violent? Or had Sheila interrupted a random break-in? The article reported no evidence of theft, but Hedy, of course, would bring up home invasions, and then illegal immigrants.

I found Doris Carney's telephone number in the Oberlin Home Pages and dialed it. An answering machine picked up so I left a short message, remembering Sheila's plans for a cook-out only five days ago. *Frantic* was probably the mildest word for Doris Carney. Then I phoned Theo, who'd just read the news. He insisted I drop by for a drink after work. To my surprise, he even offered to go out for pizza.

After forcing myself through the day, with Sheila on my mind, I arrived at Theo's, too late for the six o'clock TV news. He greeted me with a tight face. "Come, meet Stavro," he said, in a dispirited tone. "I called Daphne about the shooting. She liked Sheila, you know, so they dropped by. I've got some wine in the fridge, you must need a drink. I certainly do."

In the living room Daphne stood by a stocky man in his late sixties. She was adjusting her neck scarf, one of those fancy French numbers sporting a bold pattern of horseshoes.

"We just got here," she called, hurrying over to my side. The dark man stepped up next to her. "This is my fiancé," she said.

As we shook hands I felt sorry for Theo. Stavro had presence. He wasn't fat, just substantial – a European man. He wouldn't be boisterous or arrogant, but he knew his own worth, and patience might not be one of his virtues. He and Daphne settled on the sofa and I noticed her reach over to pat his thigh. "I've always liked Sheila," she said.

"I didn't know her," Stavro offered, as if we needed a reason for his silence. He had a stern face but alert amused eyes.

Daphne was now leaning towards him, preoccupied, so I followed Theo into the kitchen and sat on one of the wrought-iron chairs at his glass-topped table, the morning's *Chronicle* folded in half on a cloth placemat.

"No updates about Sheila," he said, taking wine glasses from a cupboard. "I wonder where the paper found her picture?"

Not a word about his sister. Theo handed me a glass of wine and settled on an opposite chair.

"Shouldn't we join them?" I asked.

"In a minute. I phoned my lawn guys this afternoon. They'll look after the garden now. What are you going to do? I mean…"

"I can't think about that," I interrupted.

"Didn't she hang around with some creepy guy?" Said without irony or self-awareness. "You get on with her better than I do."

I nursed my white wine, not up for pleasantries with Daphne and Stavro.

"You know how she always has an eye out for free things," Theo continued. "I have a dozen bricks in the garage and she wanted those for her garden, for some border, but I told her I might use them, too."

"C'mon, Theo, that's just Sheila. And in spite of all her money worries, she's been feeding her neighborhood's stray cats."

We had an entire conversation without Theo mentioning Neil even once, while Daphne and Stavro cooled their heels. Then, after a round a drinks with them, and some genial but pointless talk, I headed home. Mrs. Carney had left a message on my answering machine, asking me to phone her the next morning; ominously, nothing more. There was also an invitation from Claire Warren to her annual June bash – the party I no longer attended. But she knew I wouldn't show up, and that wasn't the real reason for her call. "Everyone at the mall's aghast about Sheila," she went on in one of her interminable messages. Claire had said she'd seen her there the day before and they'd commiserated about poor sales; they'd even joked about checking out obituaries in anticipation of promising estate sales. Finally, she got around to asking if I'd heard any news about Guy's Beecher Stowe's letters.

That night I dreamed of the antique mall. Without consulting me, the college had purchased it as an annex to the archive, and somehow attached it. I could step through the walls the way dreamers do, drifting effortlessly from book-filled library stacks to the booths that lined the mall's aisles. But to my surprise most of them had been emptied. Sheila's booth, however, was just as I remembered, the blue-white oriental vase she'd turned into a lamp in its customary place on a kidney-shaped art deco dressing table. Someone had put yellow police tape around the booth yet I could enter at will. A large glass case held Sheila's inventory of arts-and-crafts pottery – her Roseville, Weller, Rookwood and McCoy. As my right hand, transparent, reached for its door, I heard a commotion behind me. And then, waking, I was overwhelmed with a sense of desolation.

The Saturday papers rehashed Sheila's attack, along with irrelevant articles about antiquing in Ohio, and speculations about rivalries between dealers who were all after illusive treasures. They liked the idea that Sheila might have been shot by another dealer. When I finally reached Doris Carney, she sounded confused. Sheila was in our local hospital, and if her doctors could be trusted, the bullet hadn't punctured an organ. Doris gave me her own cell phone number and said to visit Sheila "ASAP."

I set my conference paper aside. At some point during the weekend, Sheila would have appeared to fuss over the garden and we'd have continued our talks. Even if she snapped at me,

I'd come to count on her presence; her gentleness was lavished only on plants.

After a quick lunch I headed over to the Mercy Allen Hospital, a two-storied, seventies, tan brick pile on West Lorain Street that might have been attached to a shopping center. I peeked into the Gift Shop – no fresh flowers – and took the elevator across from it to the patients' rooms on the second floor.

Sheila looked almost comfortable in her hospital bed in a private room. Her left arm was connected to an IV at the wrist, but her hair had just been brushed or combed.

"They were supposed to take this damn contraption off hours ago," she said. "I sent Mother to get one of the nurses, I've had enough. She thinks there should be an armed guard outside my door but I keep telling her I'm not a celebrity."

"You'll do anything for a rest," I tried to joke, for some lightness. "So, what happened?"

"I was shot in the ass!"

"What?"

"You heard me. In my ass! Can you believe it?"

"Slow down, Sheila. How's that possible? Your mother said…"

"Well, it happened. There's a fancy medical name, and they call it the 'buttock fold,' but it's my ass. Right before it hits the back of the thigh."

"That must be painful."

"The bullet penetrated dermis – another one of their words – but fortunately not muscle." She began to laugh with a desperate edge. "You know, after a certain age a woman has to choose between her face and her butt. Carrying an extra ten pounds is better for the face, you won't look gaunt, so it's lucky that was my choice."

"Let's go back to last night and start at the beginning."

"I've already told every cop in town. I was in the basement, getting stuff ready for the mall, when I heard a noise above me. In the living room. At first I figured it must be the cats chasing each other, but I didn't call out to stop, I didn't want to make matters worse. They're sensitive, and they don't listen anyway. But when I came upstairs I saw two creeps near the fireplace. They had on those ski masks that cover the face, you know, and one was carrying a cloth bag that looked like a pillowcase. You can imagine how pissed I was. So I screamed, 'What the fuck are you doing?' and grabbed the back of the dining-room chair. I was gonna go after the short one with the chair, and the other one, the taller one, pulled his gun – it was two guys, of course – and then I don't know exactly what went on but I heard a bang and next thing I was on the floor and the front door slammed."

"You could've been killed!"

"Sure. And I'll bet those guys know Loretta."

"Oh, Sheila, they might've been anyone. Your neighbors see you going in and out all the time with antiques, maybe…"

"Will you do a couple favors for me?"

"If I can."

"First, I'd like you to call the police."

"What for?"

"You know all about Loretta. I need you to tell them about her. In case they think I'm a nut."

"But why do you think Loretta has anything to do with it?"

"If you don't want to help me just say so."

Sheila usually had better street smarts. "I'll phone them, sure, but it won't do any good."

"Okay, you can do it from here. Use my cell phone."

"And then what?"

"Just phone them. When you're done I'll tell you."

I dialed from her cell, and in no time a receptionist took my call, put me on hold, and then transferred me to someone named Lieutenant Foley. After identifying myself, I mentioned Sheila's late-night harassment, her troubles with Brad and her fear of Loretta. The voice at the other end of the line was steady and encouraging. He urged me to keep in contact with Mrs. Carney because she'd been *very distressed* – his words. I gave him my telephone numbers at home and at the college, just in case. In case of what, I didn't know.

When I finished, Sheila seemed relieved. "Now you'll hate this, but I can't ask anyone else. Take my mother to church. She's too strung out and she really needs the afternoon mass." She grinned for a second. "The Saturday Old People's Mass, that's what we call it. And I'd like to be by myself. I'm really not her little girl anymore, I need some rest from her."

This wasn't what I expected. "If it'll help you," I agreed, not mentioning the chapel downstairs.

During our drive, Mrs. Carney chattered away, oblivious to anything but her daughter. Orange day lilies already bloomed along the roadside, a month too early. Sheila had no use for them – "they're almost weeds," she often said – when they opened by my garage, but I refused to let her dig them up. Their soft apricot petals, streaked with burnt orange, meant high summer to me, and the freedom of childhood's long school vacations.

Set back from the road at the edge of town, in an expanse of grass that resembled a golf course, Sacred Heart had been built in the 1950s. Originally a social hall, it was converted when the parish couldn't raise enough money for another new church. The addition of stained-glass windows – bright abstract designs, each relating a parable – gave it a fanciful air.

"Is this your church, too?" Mrs. Carney asked, as I pulled into the parking lot.

"No," I said. "I don't have a church. But I've been here several times. For a colleague's wedding and a few funerals."

"I prefer the old churches," she said.

I walked beside her and she matched her step to mine.

I didn't say that my mother had been buried from this church, or that memories of her funeral service were filling my head. It had taken place on a bitter November morning fifteen years ago, yet like yesterday. We'd had early snow flurries but both Nick and Hedy stood by me, though they'd been worried about the drive. *Don't go there*, I warned myself.

We made our way through the parking lot, then the foyer. I reached for a weekly bulletin, for anything to read, and looked about. Perhaps two dozen people filled the pews, nearly all over seventy. Mrs. Carney pointed at one of the old plaster statues that must have been set out to soften the church's modern lines. Sunlight poured through the glittering windows and I tried to guess which parable was illustrated by a particularly beautiful blue blob. Chartres blue, I think it's called. If you squinted, you could almost see it was the one about the mustard seed.

"That's my favorite window," Mrs. Carney whispered.

Several late-comers stopped to light votive candles beneath the sandaled feet of a large plaster Jesus. I turned to another window's puzzle when I heard movement in the foyer.

"They're starting up," she said.

I hoped she wouldn't offer a running commentary.

"Sometimes that's the best part, I'm not tired yet. All that kneeling later on, you know. The ups and downs."

Despite her chatter, a look of panic remained on her face, and her eyes were red; she'd had quite a scare. Was she imagining her daughter's casket near the altar, draped with a spray of pink roses?

Behind us, a gruff woman's voice said, "But I told her you don't *have* to get married."

"Ssshh," her companion whispered.

I tried to lose myself in the newsletter, though it wasn't working, and started to wonder what Hedy would make of all this.

"Don't you shush me," came from behind.

Three

Which of you shall have a friend and shall go unto him
at midnight and say unto him, Friend, lend me three loaves.
And he from within shall answer and say, Trouble me not:
the door is now shut; I cannot rise and give thee.
I say unto you, though he will not rise and give him,
because he is his friend, yet because of his importunity
he will rise and give him as many as he needeth.

—LUKE, XI, V-VIII

18

For a long time I thought this was the story of my friends. Now, I see that it belongs to me, too. It's also the story of my failure to stand up to them, to speak out sooner and risk the loss of friendship. There's plenty of evasion and lack of trust to go around. Maybe nothing would be different today, maybe we would have stopped speaking years ago, but I'll never know. It's hindsight, yes, though still true.

"We heard about Sheila," Hedy said flatly, as we settled at the picnic table behind the Antons' garage. "I'm sorry. We know you like her."

Nick nodded while she spoke. They were of one accord.

"It's such a violent world," she added, shaking her head.

We'd come outside to admire the butterfly garden Nick had recently planted for Hedy on a spot where crab apples had dropped last fall. He'd cleared a twelve-foot square and staked the small low plants at one-foot intervals, almost like a vegetable plot. In a few months it would be worth seeing, if the local deer didn't finish it off first.

Hedy was willing their lives back to some kind of routine. Since our last visit she'd been searching out estate sales and had also gone to several evening auctions. Somehow she would lead Nick into the future. And with speculations about the upcoming fall election louder each day now, I could expect more grievances from the Antons.

"The mall contacted us," Nick said. "They want all dealers to check their booths for missing items."

"But it doesn't sound like anyone from the mall was involved." We'd carried glasses of iced tea with us. It was a day of relentless sun.

"You never know," he replied. "We have to do an inventory, and that's a big job."

"Did you hear from the police? They're speaking to everyone who might have seen Sheila recently."

"At least she's still alive," Hedy said. "That's karma for you."

"Some karma," I said, immediately regretting my words. I didn't want to spoil the afternoon before starting out. We'd planned a country drive with a little antiquing for good measure. Today, as I write this, I see that I was playing a make-believe game with myself, holding onto the past.

"I wouldn't want to be shot." Hedy's right hand touched her heart.

"Don't think about Sheila, hon," Nick said protectively, and then turned to me. "Hedy's so sensitive, you know that. She feels things deeply."

"I know," I agreed.

"Hey, fellas, don't talk about me like I'm not here."

"You're right," I said, though she appeared to be pleased by Nick's words. "Her mother's pretty upset. Last week I drove her to mass, she couldn't make it alone."

"I didn't think Sheila was Catholic."

Hedy had been raised as a Methodist, and claimed it didn't take.

"She was very fond of Guy."

Both my friends bristled. "I've asked Nick to write a poem about him," Hedy observed, smiling at her husband. "Just for me. Great poems can come from grief."

"That makes sense," I said. "Did you know that Sheila helped paint Guy's kitchen cupboards before he moved in?"

"No, I didn't," Hedy replied, raising an eyebrow.

"She often speaks of Guy." I was testing the water. "Since his death."

"Guy liked everyone at the mall," Nick said.

"She was quite impressed by his Civil War collection."

"I didn't know she was interested in the Civil War," Hedy said skeptically.

What, I wondered, was going on in Nick's head. I thought of Guy's proud grin as he showed me his rented house, his first place of his own. "She and Guy talked about it a lot."

Nick leaned forward, his expression intent.

"He told her all about his summer vacations with your mother, and the battlefields they saw together."

"Oh, God," Nick groaned.

Hedy had a way of arching an eyebrow that gave me pause. "What?" she asked.

"Maybe I shouldn't have mentioned it. Those restaurant glasses I packed..."

"It's my mother," Nick said, a deep line crossing his forehead.

"You don't know the whole story," Hedy said. She lifted her chin and looked me straight in the eyes. "You don't know the half of it."

"She was impossible," Nick explained. "I've told you that before. Manipulative and self-centered. The worst prima donna. Well, there's more. She loved to interfere with people, to push them around. She liked things her way. When we bought this place she helped us out with some money. Some of it was a loan, some a gift. I shouldn't have trusted her. I should have known better, but I wanted the best for my family. Then she started on Guy, influencing him away from us. When we share our beliefs with others it's for their benefit, they're free to believe what they want. My mother couldn't accept that."

"I suppose some grandparents…" I began to say.

"It was awful," Hedy cut me short. "Questioning our values. We couldn't trust her." She reached for Nick's hand. "Sometimes when Nick's asleep he's still fighting with her. I can tell from the way he's tossing, from the sounds he makes. She was a powerful woman."

"That's why she hated Hedy," Nick said. "My wife saw through her. It's been twenty years since we spoke with her last, but some nights it's like yesterday. We had to get Guy away from her, she'd gone too far."

"I don't understand." I leaned my elbows against the table's edge, and my eyes moved back and forth from Hedy to Nick.

For a brief moment Hedy looked up into the sun. "One year, after he came back from their summer visit, we told him she'd died."

"She wasn't dead?" I paused to take it in. I must have sounded unsympathetic because they glanced at each other.

"You don't understand her power," Hedy said. "It was just after Labor Day. Guy was back in school and we'd had enough."

Nick took over. "I told her never to contact us again, that she was finished with me. And that's how we went on. We got an unlisted phone number and watched for the mail in case she wrote to Guy."

As we talked they became increasingly agitated. "She sent a few cards," Hedy reminded him. "For Guy's birthday and Christmas. But I destroyed every one. It was for the best."

"And all these years he thought she was dead?"

"There was nothing else for him to think," Hedy said.

"But you've always said she was dead."

"Dead to me," Nick hedged. "And when we stopped hearing, she might as well have been."

"I don't know what to say. It's out of some Greek tragedy."

"That's not the end of it," Nick said, a quaver in his voice. "Should I tell him?" he asked Hedy, his tone of voice dropping softly.

Him again. Like I wasn't sitting across the table less than three feet away.

Hedy swallowed her distress. "It doesn't matter."

"My mother's still alive," he continued. "I heard from her last month. She was looking up old friends on the internet, googling names from the past, and some fool e-mailed her back. That's the down side of the internet, there's no privacy. And she's found out about Guy, so she wants to see me."

"I told Nick to do what he needs to. I was always prepared to get along with her. But I don't want to dig up the past." Hedy turned to her husband.

"It's buried. I'm done with it. I told you that."

"Maybe she's ill," I suggested. "She must be over eighty by now."

"She's big trouble, Hedy understands. You wouldn't think that if you met her, she can be charming. Very charming. She must have run out of people to torment."

I began to recall Nick's stories about his mother. She had married young, fresh out of high school, and given up her dream of singing in a nightclub when he was born. A common tale from the fifties, including her lack of real talent. With hair peroxided in a starlet's style, she'd often lamented her unused gifts. Nick once thought her beautiful, and had been a devoted son.

They'd lied to me for years. To everyone, maybe even themselves – no, I doubted that. And not a bland white lie, but a whopper.

"She's probably a psychopath," Hedy suggested. "We've read books about psychopaths, trying to understand her."

151

"She was jealous of Hedy from the first day."

"I felt it immediately," she explained, watching her husband intently. "The way she looked me over. Nick warned me but I couldn't believe it. After we got married, I usually stayed home when Nick went for a visit. When Guy was born she seemed to soften around him, then she married again and we thought maybe she'd changed."

"We were so relieved when she moved to Knoxville," Nick said. "But she charmed Guy by telephone, she'd send him cards and presents. He thought she was special and we didn't want to upset him."

None of this sounded sinister, even unusual, but my friends' faces were filled with pain and anger.

"You don't know what she could be like." Hedy's remark was quick. "One summer she drove north for a visit. She stayed with some friends, said she didn't want to be a burden, and then started in on Guy, taking him out for day trips, buying little gifts. The ideal grandmother. We could hardly object. It seemed innocent at first. And one night he came home from an outing – they'd been to an amusement park – and he said she'd invited him to drive back to Knoxville with her, for an adventure."

"He wouldn't let go of it, he'd been seduced." Nick paused for a moment and closed his eyes briefly. "We asked ourselves what harm it would do, she was his only living grandparent, he didn't have any brothers or sisters. We were trapped."

"So, we let him go," Hedy said. "And of course the next year he wanted to go again. It was just for a month, how could we object? We should have but we didn't. She filled his head with nonsense but we didn't stop it."

"What nonsense?" I asked.

"Gradually Guy withdrew from us," Hedy continued vehemently. "His grades fell, and he was always restless – you know teenage boys are unhappy. They have to rebel."

Just listen, I told myself. Keep still.

"That's part of growing up," Hedy allowed. "We shouldn't have let him go but it was the one thing he wanted. And when he came back he announced that he was moving to Knoxville, he wanted to live with Nick's mother. Well, that was the end. I wasn't going to give her my son."

"Is that when you told him she'd died?"

"It had to stop. It was hard on us, but it had to end," Hedy said, flustered.

"And he believed you?"

"I'm sure he did." Nick said. "We monitored the phone and watched the mail. For a year we even had it delivered to a post-box so nothing would slip by us. We did everything possible. Everything."

"And she never tried…"

"Just more cards." Hedy spoke again, as if they were taking turns. "Then we told her that we'd get a restraining order, we'd talk to a lawyer. We couldn't let her destroy our family."

While they talked, Sheila's account of Guy's confession never left my thoughts. This morning I'd promised myself to avoid dangerous topics but I wasn't prepared for a story like this one.

"It was a horrible time," Nick said. "We're old-fashioned, you know that. Guy was our son, our family. We had to protect him. That's what…"

"That's what we believe," Hedy added. "Marriage and the family. We want to be free to live our values. We don't force them on anyone else."

They often finished each other's sentences with such ease I half imagined them preparing for a visit: "You say *this*, I'll say *that*."

"Just free," she muttered, as if she never expected to feel that way again.

"But no one's stopping you," I objected.

"Don't you believe in liberty?" Nick continued.

We were shifting gear fast, a bad move.

"You've asked me that before. It's a question that sets you up as moral arbiter of the world – or at least this discussion – and it can't be answered without…"

"I don't see why not."

"If we're going to talk seriously, we have to apply the same set of standards to both sides of the argument."

"Not if you think one side is completely wrong," Hedy corrected me.

"Look, there are things you value. Things that matter to you…"

"Yes?" she asked.

I should have quit there, but couldn't. "Take your diet, for instance. You see it as moral. A moral choice. Okay, that's fine, I respect you for it. But it's not for everyone. Remember Hitler didn't eat meat, and wouldn't touch booze. He was a vegetarian, too, but a tyrant. Morality's not so easy."

"What a rotten example!" Nick protested. "Plucking Hitler out of the air is a cheap trick."

"It's true, though. Maybe he's an extreme example, but you often take extreme positions."

They both glared at me, our friendship on the line.

I'd better be the appeaser. "Look, forget about Hitler, okay? He's not the point. Just my bad choice, sorry. But none of us has the corner on virtue."

We were talking past each other, as usual. This was no afternoon for antiquing, I wanted only an escape. People fell out with old friends and I saw this was happening to me. I'd known Hedy since we were fourteen and our bond was fast unraveling.

"He's forgotten," Hedy said with a hard smile. I imagined her teeth were clenched.

19

Monday, June 11

My visit with the Antons bothered me all weekend, like a festering sore. If friendship means you have to keep a list of subjects to avoid, if politics and religion and anything worth talking about are off limits, then the bond's just a habit. An affectionate one, sure, but you may as well stay in your room by yourself.

When I arrived at work, relieved to be back in my office, a message from Lieutenant Foley flashed on my answering machine. Would I please call him? It wasn't urgent, he added. Just a few questions. He had a casual but efficient manner, like someone taking a delivery order for groceries.

We finally spoke before lunch, and he asked if I knew anything about Sheila's connection to Guy. Caught off guard, I must have hesitated, because he asked me to drop by the police station that afternoon. When I mentioned helping Mrs. Carney and Sheila with her mall inventory that evening, I could almost feel him push the receiver closer to his ear. "We'd better talk before that," he said. Detective work, I was beginning to see, resembled archival work – you had the evidence at hand, and questions about it. You had to make sense of facts once you knew what they were.

The Oberlin Police Department is located behind the municipal court building on South Main, a brisk five-minute walk from Gibson's and a block from the Lorain County

Coroner's Office. At first you might miss its entrance unless you knew where you're going.

I'd once read that the police force has twenty-five full-time officers, but the space seemed too small for all of them at the same time. While waiting in the lobby I stood before two large vending machines filled with candy, chips, salted nuts and soft drinks. There was no place to sit so you couldn't comfortably enjoy your junk food – that might, in fact, have been the point. Yet three teenage boys stood outside, by the entrance, munching on chips. This corner of the lobby could belong to any college campus.

Lieutenant Foley soon joined me. A barrel-chested man in his early forties, with a recent buzz cut, he motioned me into a small windowless anteroom off the lobby. "Is this okay?" he asked in a gracious tone.

"It's fine," I said, and sat across from him, knowing little about police procedures.

"Are you a close friend of the Carney family?"

"Not close, but more than a good acquaintance." I wasn't splitting hairs even if it sounded like that. A pad and pen had already been set on the table between us.

"Does Ms. Carney tend to exaggerate?"

"Sheila can be colorful, but I've never known her to lie. Are you thinking of her complaints about her ex-boyfriend?"

"We could start there."

I told him what I knew, which amounted to very little.

"We know she's not lying," he said softly, as if to reassure me.

"And she isn't trying to get even with Brad for leaving her. They were on-and-off for five years. Recently, mostly off."

"A habit," he observed.

"You could call it that." Suddenly I felt on display. "I've never met Loretta."

He nodded. "We're in touch with them. Had she known Guy Anton a long time?"

Apparently the police weren't concerned about Brad or Loretta, or that's what he wanted me to think.

"More than ten years." I gave him the history. All of it.

"And you believed Ms. Carney's story?"

I didn't reply at once. I hadn't meant to speak out.

"About Guy Anton's father?" he persisted.

"I don't like to. I warned her about false memories, but she was certain. She thought Guy might've kept a journal – his therapist had encouraged it – though I didn't find one. Was it in his car? Or on his computer? Maybe I shouldn't ask."

He smiled and shook his head. A noncommital response, or a denial? I was starting to second-guess the police. As yet he'd written nothing on his pad.

"There's one thing I just learned this weekend. I feel like I'm betraying a confidence, but Guy's grandmother isn't dead. He loved visiting her when he was a teenager but she's not dead, like he thought."

Foley's eyes narrowed. "Do you know where she is?"

"No idea. And she married a second time so I'm not even sure of her name."

"How do you know all this?"

"The Antons told me. Nick did. Just the other day. His mother had e-mailed him after years of being estranged. She'd heard about Guy's death."

"You get around," Foley said, smiling. "A lot of people seem connected to you. You're friends with Neil Breuler, too."

"He rents a room from an old friend, but you know that. Neil's barely an acquaintance. I saw them together one night on Tappan Square. Guy and Neil. A couple days before Guy's fall. And a few weeks ago he came to my office on campus, he wanted to know if Guy's parents had heard about him. He was worried that his wife's divorce lawyer might hear about his affair. I really don't know what went on between them. Guy never told me."

Lieutenant Foley nodded again and scribbled something on the pad. A clever man, he'd known how to get me to talk.

"Do you mind if I ask a few questions?"

"Why not?" he said amiably, with half a chuckle, yet his eyes were shrewd.

"I can't figure out…" I stopped to collect my thoughts. I was saying too much and drew back. "It's pretty strange, talking like this about people I care for."

"You've done the right thing. We're looking at all angles. We might need to call on you again. You have a good reputation at the college, I made a few queries."

Best ignore that remark.

"If you hear anything unusual tonight…"

"Of course," I agreed, catching his drift. So, I had allied myself with the police – sort of. Yet I felt sullied by our meeting, and angry with myself. What kind of choice had I made?

An hour later, when I arrived at the mall, a sign on the door asked dealers to leave their inventory reports at the main desk. Sheila and her mother hadn't yet appeared, and I hoped nothing was wrong. I'd offered to take them to a restaurant afterward but Doris declined: "I don't like restaurants. There are too many choices and the food's usually a disappointment. Or it makes me sick." All things considered, this struck me as a reasonable reply. On my way to Sheila's booth, I kept an eye out for the Antons.

"Hey, hey!" Claire Warren stood checking book titles against a pegboard. "I didn't expect to see you."

The mall was busier than I'd anticipated, and when I mentioned this, Claire snorted, "The gawkers, they're out for a thrill – people love a mystery. What's going on with you?"

"I'm helping with Sheila's inventory."

"Good luck. I didn't think Sheila would be up to that yet. She knows every particle of dust here. I was terrified to come by today."

"But nothing happened here. And you're surrounded by people."

Claire laughed. "You don't think people are terrifying?"

"I never expected to hear you say anything like that."

"Then you underestimate me. I'd be glad to help out," Claire said, "but there's a reception tonight for a retiring dean, an old pal. There are days when I wonder if I should keep my booth. With internet everything's on-line, and most business is out-of-state. I'm just nostalgic about the mall, I've been here so long I can't give it up. But I don't need to put my life at risk to sell a few old books." She set down her pegboard. "Sheila and I, we're not close. She's a man's woman, you know what I mean. But she works hard. My garden already misses her."

"I forgot she does your garden, too."

"I try to imagine what happened, but I can't."

"What are the other dealers saying?"

"No one knows what to think. Or who's next…"

Claire stopped in mid-sentence as Doris Carney headed down the aisle toward us. In her pink T-shirt, jeans and white baseball cap, she might have come from doing the laundry, but she'd dabbed herself with a sweet floral perfume as if for a night on the town. Claire immediately put her arms around Mrs. Carney and the two women commiserated while I scouted out Sheila's booth.

"I don't think I can do an inventory tonight," Doris sighed.

Claire began to stroke her shoulder. "There's no hurry," she said.

"I'm sorry to waste your time."

"Please don't think that," I said. "We'll just have dinner. I've already made it."

In a few moments Sheila joined us, looking in better shape than I expected, although she carried an old wooden cane in her left hand.

"We're not working tonight," Doris announced. "We're just having dinner. We need a good time."

Sheila didn't object, which surprised me, and, with a sullen expression, said, "Whatever."

When we arrived at my place, Doris said she was ready for a glass of wine. I'd set the dining-room table that morning, and dinner only needed heating up. The food doesn't matter, but I remembered Doris's dentures while shopping for it. Sheila carried her cane to the table and hung it on the back of her chair.

"What happened to your cats?" I asked her, an easy beginning as we settled at the table.

"One of my friends took them home for now," Mrs. Carney said. "I already have three of my own. If you add one here and one there, soon you're running a cat motel. I told Sheila to watch out or she'll end up a crazy cat lady."

I knew from Sheila that Doris only liked Gallo Chablis, and filled her glass. She watched me carefully. "Don't let me go beyond three glasses. I'm driving, and that's my limit. I told Sheila to sell everything to another dealer. We could move to Florida. To the sun."

Sheila kept silent. That didn't sound like a plan of hers.

The police had allowed Sheila back into her house as soon as the hospital discharged her, as she'd insisted, although Lieutenant Foley didn't strike me as someone easily intimidated.

"I never expected anything like this to happen," Mrs. Carney went on.

We both turned to Sheila, who seemed lost in her own thoughts. Then I saw she wasn't smoking. Sheila usually had a cigarette going, sometimes even while she ate.

"Oh, we have our differences, and I can bug her, but that's how it is. I'm not the easiest person to get along with. That's why I prefer my cats."

"Like Sheila," I said.

"Truer words…" Mrs. Carney – I still had trouble thinking of her as Doris – looked down at her plate and picked up a fork. "I never eat cucumber," she said, pushing some slices aside on her salad plate. "It doesn't agree with me."

"That's alright. I can't eat raw green pepper."

She made an effort to smile. "Me neither."

"I eat them both," Sheila said finally, rousing herself.

When Sheila's in a funk, she hates questions about it. Best keep on talking to her mother. "Did you hear anything more about Guy Anton from your friend? His landlady."

"She didn't know the family, but Sheila calls them monsters."

"I've known his mother since the ninth grade."

"Well, Sheila calls a lot of people monsters. She's always angry. Like me. And there's a lot to be angry about out there. I tell myself it's just politics but…"

"Politics is us, Doris, that's the trouble."

"What do you mean?"

"What happens, on all sides, that's who we are."

Sheila focused on her salad with an intent expression that baffled me.

"You don't seem the angry type," Doris said.

"I keep it to myself."

"So, we're all alike. You should have a cat," she suggested.

I laughed. "I don't know about that."

"I'm serious. You're missing something."

"We're all missing something, don't you think?"

Now Sheila laughed too, but with a bitter edge.

"Did you tell your mother about Guy?" I hoped this was a safe question.

"She told me what his father had done. I'm a big girl but it makes me sick."

I resisted the impulse to defend Nick. Sometimes I hold on too long. Isn't that what Theo called me – a dog with a bone?

"He ought to be punished," Sheila added. "The prick."

"But there's no way to prove it," I said. Sheila's mood was getting to me. She seemed ready to lash out at someone.

Mrs. Carney speared a piece of lettuce but didn't bring it to her mouth. "It must've happened. Sheila has a strong sense of justice, you know that. When she was little I could never take her to the zoo – she couldn't stand seeing animals in a cage."

I filled our wine glasses again. "That's number two, Doris." I sounded like a stern parent. "Do you want more wine?" I asked Sheila, and she held her glass out to me.

"And it drove her crazy when a cat caught a bird – she couldn't stand that," Mrs. Carney added, smiling at her daughter.

"That's enough," Sheila said. "Okay? That's enough!"

"Maybe that's why you got involved with Brad," Mrs. Carney rambled on. "He was like a wounded animal."

What's going on here? I wondered, and then it hit me. Sheila probably hadn't heard from Brad since the shooting. He'd ignored her crisis.

"But wounded animals sometimes attack," I said.

"She's too good for him, she was always saving him. Eventually people resent that."

Sheila glowered at me and slumped over her plate.

"Funny, Doris, but I've said that too."

20

I didn't expect to hear from Lieutenant Foley again soon, yet there was a phone message from him when I got to my office after a staff meeting. My dinner with Sheila and Mrs. Carney had yielded little to tell.

"There's someone I'd like you to meet," the lieutenant said when we connected. "You wouldn't by any chance be able to come by this morning?"

I offered to walk over on my lunch hour.

"We'll be waiting," he replied.

After hanging up I regretted not going at once. It must be strange being a cop and seeing mostly the worst in people. Archival work at least can give you hope. But some days I think I live in a time that has run out of hope, a time that's forgotten how to remember the past.

Again, my wait in the lobby was brief, and Lieutenant Foley escorted me down a long corridor to a larger office than the anteroom where we'd last talked. It had a window, and an elderly woman sitting across from the desk. "I want to introduce you to Mrs. Roberts."

"Annie Roberts," she said. "Just plain Annie."

"Nick Anton's mother," the lieutenant explained. "I told her about you, and she asked to meet you."

Hell, what was I in for?

"I did," she concurred. "The lieutenant's very thoughtful."

Patches of scalp showed through her thin blondish white hair, and the powdery mask applied to her face needed refreshing. At first I saw no resemblance to Nick, only a frail old woman in a lime-green pantsuit. She wore more rings than I could bother to count.

"I thought you might prefer meeting here," he said. "In my office."

If this was his space, it gave little away about its occupant. Some file folders had been piled neatly on the desk by a day book, stacked edge to edge, but there were no framed photographs, nothing personal. Only an empty coffee mug with the college's logo, which I didn't expect to see in the police department. Of course I had no reason to expect anything. And then I noticed a small paper bag that looked suspiciously like it held doughnuts from Gibson's.

"I'm glad you could come," Mrs. Roberts – Annie – said.

"I'll leave the two of you," Foley offered. "Take your time."

When he turned to go, we looked at each other hesitantly. "Thank you, officer," Mrs Roberts called to him as he closed the door.

"I wonder if he's bugging us?" she asked immediately.

"Beats me," I said. "Why would he want to do that?"

"I don't know what you've heard about me, but I've been trying to talk to my son. He's always been stubborn, and when I phoned the police here this nice man told me you'd been helpful to them, you knew Guy and his family."

I was wary but hooked. "That's true."

"Now I've got a little problem. You see, my son and I haven't spoken for twenty years, and he won't respond to my phone calls or e-mails."

"You must feel awful, but what can I do?"

"Well, dear, it's like this. I want to see my son."

"I don't think I can help."

"Now just hear me out."

"I'm listening. Really."

"That's so nice of you. I mean it. I don't know where else to turn. Ever since I learned about Guy's death I've been sick at heart. You have to believe me. He was a darling boy and I've never forgiven my son for keeping me from him all these years."

"What was it about?" I couldn't resist asking.

"I have a big personality – that's what my last husband used to say. And I don't think Nicky liked it. I know his wife didn't. But I'm just a mother. Families put things aside. That's no reason to disown your mother, don't you think?"

I nodded along with her.

"I loved Guy. I was probably a better grandmother than a mother. Did Nicky ever talk about me?"

Those large dark eyes might have been her son's. "A little."

"Oh," she said, "come on, dear."

"This is very awkward. Why don't you call him again?"

"He won't answer. I told you he's stubborn. And that wife of his…"

"She's a very old friend of mine. Since we were fourteen."

She blanched, then conceded, "She was a pretty one. Very pretty. Nicky always liked that. But I don't want to talk about her. She distracted him from his studies and ruined his career, though that's all yesterday. When I learned about Guy I cried and cried. Believe it or not, I loved that boy. And he loved me."

"I know."

"You do? How?"

"When Guy rented a house not far from here I visited him, and he told me about his trips to Knoxville, how you piqued his interest in the Civil War."

"We watched my tape of *Gone With the Wind* every visit. We'd make a pan of fudge…"

"He didn't tell me that."

"Well, we did."

"I packed up his things after he died, and he had some drinking glasses from a restaurant in Georgia. I gave them to Hedy."

"Aunt Fanny's Cabin? He loved that place. I'd like one of their mint juleps right now. I had four visits from Guy, each one for a month. It was almost like…" she stopped.

"Like what?"

"Like having Nicky back as a boy." She took a tissue from her purse and wiped her eyes. "I won't cry, I promise. Do they still have that guru of theirs?"

I nodded.

"Guy, too?"

"Yes."

"Oh dear. You know Nicky was raised Catholic but he never had much interest in religion. He was like me. When I married his father, Joe Antonacci, I had to convert, my family were Baptists. But I always liked Italian men. Sinatra, Dean Martin, Vic Damone. They always did it for me. So I told Joey I'd go along with him, I'd raise our kids anyway he wanted. He wasn't religious himself, but his family, well, is the pope Catholic?

"I remember one time his sister came to our house with this big framed photograph of the pope. Pius whatever. He had a number and a sour face, that one. Joey wanted to hang it in the dining room, right where we ate, but I said no way, I wasn't having it. But he was scared of his family, he didn't like arguments, and he hung it anyway. So the next day I went to the dime-store and bought a nice picture frame, not as fancy as the pope's but painted gold, and I cut a page out of *Photoplay*, a good picture of Elvis Presley, and put it in the frame and nailed it to the wall, up there by that other one. Elvis and Pius, hanging together. You should have seen Joey's face. And I said, 'Both of them go or both stay.'"

As we laughed together, I realized I was starting to like her. Nick had been right – she could be charming.

"And they were gone before his family came over again. Poor Joey. Now Mr. Roberts, he wasn't Italian, but he was nice to me. And he adored Guy. He never had kids of his own and he thought the world of Guy."

"You tell a good story, Mrs. Roberts."

"It's all true. When Joey died – Nicky was nine or ten, I forget which – he said he didn't want to get up early for church anymore, and I certainly didn't, so that was it for religion. He'd gone through all that first communion stuff, I still have his picture, but from then on we only went to church at Christmas and Easter. And I liked it that way. Did he ever tell you that?"

"I don't remember. I don't think so. I knew he'd been raised Catholic."

"What else did they tell you about me?"

"Not much. Really. I hate to say this but for years I thought you were dead."

She winced. "It's terrible, what they did to me. She was behind it."

"What went wrong, Mrs. Roberts? You must have some idea."

I often wished my parents were still alive, so Nick's obstinacy made little sense.

"The first time Guy came to Knoxville he was curious and lively, the ideal grandson. The next visits, too. But when he turned thirteen it was like another person was growing inside him. Some mornings I'd find him staring into space like he didn't know where he was."

"A moody boy?"

"I figured it must be his glands – his body was driving him nuts. I thought he'd turn into a dreamy teenager but it didn't happen. The next summer he was worse. Maybe not worse, exactly, but closed off. And sad. He was so sad. I tried to get him to talk about it, what he liked in school, what he didn't, but I couldn't get anywhere. So we drove all over looking at old battle sites, that would distract him for a while. And then one night he told me he didn't want to go home ever again, he wanted to stay with me.

"You can imagine what happened. Nicky exploded and Hedy screamed into the phone that I wasn't going to steal her son. I remember her words. But what Guy told me next made my blood boil."

"What did he say, Mrs. Roberts?"

"That a man had touched him where he shouldn't. He could barely say the words."

"Who was it?"

"He wouldn't tell me, I never knew, but I phoned Nicky and said he'd better find out what was going on. Guy was afraid to tell his parents – it must've been one of his teachers. I read Nicky the riot act but he insisted Guy was making it up and told me he'd take care of everything, that I shouldn't interfere. When Guy went home that summer he cried all the way to the airport. And he blamed me for sending him back.

"Next thing, Nicky told me I was stirring up trouble, I didn't understand Guy, and forbid me to contact him. I tried for a while but never heard back. And then Nicky said he'd hire a lawyer to keep me away from his family. My own son said that." Her eyes brimmed with tears but she ignored them. "Can you imagine? I never heard anything like it. My husband put his foot down and said we had to stay clear of them. And I gave up. I listened to him. He was my husband, and at least someone cared about me."

"I'm speechless, Mrs. Roberts."

"Annie, please. That's *my* name."

There was a knock on the door and Lieutenant Foley stepped into his office. "Can I help with anything?"

"My life's almost over, I'm eighty-three, and I want to see Nicky one more time, but I realize there's no point to it. And now that Guy's dead it's too late to fix things. I should have stayed home."

Lieutenant Foley and I looked at each other; he'd wanted me to hear this.

"You're my last chance," Annie continued, wiping her nose.

"Do you have friends here?" I asked.

"A cousin, in Lorain. I'm staying with her. She's waiting for me at the inn, we were planning to spend the night but now I just want to go home. To Knoxville. As soon as I can. I won't bother my son anymore. I lost him long ago."

"I'll drive you back to the inn," Lieutenant Foley offered gently. "This has been pretty tough."

I stood to leave with them.

"We can talk another time," he said over his shoulder, as I followed them out of his office.

The world was closing in on me. Just ask yourself, what gets you up in the morning? It has to be more than work, or duty, or love. I could almost see into the future, catch a glimpse of my life's obliteration. But I haven't yet used up my days. I felt a terrible sadness about what was going to happen, and an anger that pushed me forward, an anger for Guy, dead from a trauma to the back of his skull in a near empty basement. It was no longer possible to look away, as Nick had turned his back on his mother.

By the end of the day I wanted to hide out in my own place, but ahead was an evening at Theo's, with me as chaperone. Or buffer zone. Daphne had agreed to bring Stavro for dinner and I was meant to diffuse any tension. Apparently I'd smoothed over some rough spots at our last meeting and Theo felt grateful. As my mother used to say, no good deed goes unpunished. I brought along a bottle of white wine, and hoped to make a short night of it. I could always plead an unfinished report for an early meeting the next day.

"Theo, you're good with names," I said, while settling in one of the plaid chairs across from Daphne. "I've been trying to think of one all day but so far my mind's a blank."

"Give us a clue," Daphne said.

"She was a sixties folk singer with a husky croak."

"Odetta?" guessed Daphne.

"No. That's not it. There was a line in one of her songs that keeps going through my head: 'There's a bottom below the bottom you know.'"

"Oh, that's easy!" Theo exclaimed. "Malvina Reynolds. I had one of her albums at university. It might still be in the attic."

"I knew you'd remember."

"Theo's great with names," Daphne said to Stavro.

"I didn't think you liked folk music," I said to Theo.

"He used to have a ponytail and wear a dashiki," Daphne teased. "I'm not kidding."

"At least we weren't covered with tattoos," Theo said.

"You don't see that in Greece," Stavro joined in. "Only on garage mechanics or tourists."

There's a bottom below the bottom you know.

"Why were you thinking of Malvina?" Theo asked.

"Just that line, that's all." I didn't want to mention Lieutenant Foley. Or Nick's mother.

"It's a good one," said Stavro. "I never heard it before."

"I'd better get to the barbecue or we won't eat till midnight," Theo said, adding to me, "Want to help?"

We left Daphne and Stavro with the sherry, stopped in the kitchen for a plate of raw fish, and then headed to his backyard. "It's going well," I said. "Aren't you pleased?"

"I don't have much choice, do I?"

"Not when you put it that way."

"But I have some news. Neil's moving back. He called late last night. It's not working out with his wife. They can't stand each other. I won't say 'I told you so,' but it's okay if I think it."

"Well, you know what I think."

"Don't tell me, please. I don't like being alone, and with Daphne getting married I may as well stay put here. It only takes forty minutes to drive to her new house. And you won't believe this – it's a block away from where Sam Sheppard murdered his wife."

"I wouldn't want to live in that house."

"Oh, it was torn down long ago. I wonder where her ghost went."

"Shall we ask Daphne?" I joked.

"It might scare Stavro."

"He won't scare easily. He's not the type."

"We'll see."

"Theo, be careful." What a stupid thing for one grown man to tell another.

"I'm always careful," he replied.

Meanwhile, the salmon steaks were going to be overcooked.

When I got home that night I half-expected a message on my answering machine from Guy. Not from his ghost, just from Guy. I finally had to admit what I knew.

21

Saturday, June 16

On the morning before driving over to the Antons, I stopped at my supermarket and bought a pound of white Ranier cherries, which had just made their annual appearance. Nervous, even fearful, I didn't want to arrive empty-handed for this visit. We hadn't spoken since our awkward meeting a week ago, and Hedy hesitated when I called to say that I needed to pick up some rare books from a retired professor in Medina and could stop by for a quick cup of tea. "Around two or so, if that's okay. After lunch." Reluctantly, she agreed.

At two-fifteen I knocked on their front door. "I've rinsed the cherries, the first of the summer," I said, handing her the bag. "They're ready for eating."

Hedy made an attempt to smile. She had about her the lush scent of gardenias, her favorite.

The early afternoon sun was too hot for us to sit in their garden, so we settled in the dining room, where I set my cell phone on the table. Hedy poured the cherries into an old milk-glass bowl as Nick emerged from their kitchen.

"You've joined the twenty-first century," he said, spotting the new cell phone.

"Well, I'm too late for the twentieth."

"Do you like it? We couldn't live without ours."

"I'm not used to it yet. Next month I'm driving to Maine, and it seemed best to have one in case of any problem on the road. My car's not getting younger."

We sat around the table like old times. But it wasn't old times. Since my last visit someone had put a silver-framed studio photograph of a young boy on the buffet. It might have been Nick or Guy at six or seven, the resemblance so strong. "There's something I have to tell you," I began.

They looked at me cautiously.

"This is pretty awkward. I don't know how to start, so I'll just jump in. Yesterday I met your mother."

Apprehension clouded Nick's face, and his eyes narrowed on me.

"What are you talking about?" asked Hedy. Her eyes flitted between mine and Nick's.

"I met Nick's mother yesterday. At the police station. In Oberlin."

"At the police station?" Hedy said with a frown. "What was she doing there?"

"She'd contacted them about Guy. And the police left a message for me at work."

"Why would they call you?"

"Have you met Lieutenant Foley? He knows we're friends."

"Is my mother causing trouble?" Nick protested. He sat straighter in his chair, almost preparing for the next blow.

"She wants to see you, she told me..."

"That's not going to happen."

I looked down at the bowl of cherries. No one touched them now. Outside the dining-room window, a lone goldfinch picked at the birdfeeder, tossing seeds about as if they weren't to his taste.

"She talked about Guy," I said, "and how much she loved him."

"I still don't see why the police contacted you?" Hedy pressed. Her voice was a higher pitch than usual.

"Maybe they wanted a go-between. Someone to..."

"Is that why you're here? Nick's mother put you up to this? We warned you about her."

"I wish I'd known Guy better. I might have been able to help him."

"He didn't need your help."

Be careful, I told myself, and glanced back out the window, already regretting the fact that I'd come. I could almost swear that the goldfinch cocked its head and peered into the dining room.

"I know it's been an awful time, but does the name Neil Breuler mean anything to you?"

"Absolutely nothing," Hedy snapped. "You've asked that before. Why bring it up again?"

"You're not going to like hearing this, but there's no other way of saying it. He and Guy were having an affair."

"What?" Nick exploded. "You have a lot of nerve coming here to attack our son."

"I'm not attacking anyone. The police know all about them. And I've met the man. He's a security guard at the college."

"This is crazy," he said.

"We don't have to listen to such nonsense," Hedy added.

I think all of us knew it was too late for me to stop.

"It's nonsense," she repeated. "I'm not listening."

A look of bewilderment filled her eyes, and the air in the room had gone dead. I'll never be in this room again, I told myself.

"I don't have all the answers, but there's more to say. Neil Breuler was one of the last people to see Guy alive. The police have questioned him. I saw the two of them on Tappan Square a couple nights before Guy's death, and it looked like they'd been arguing. At first I thought one of them might be selling pot."

"Bullshit!" Nick said. "Guy didn't use drugs."

"No, you're probably right, I don't think he did."

"Then why bring it up?"

"Because the police had to rule it out."

"Was Sheila giving him pot?" Hedy asked. "I wouldn't be surprised."

"Sheila doesn't like pot. She likes beer. And cigarettes. But that's not important. Sheila was Guy's friend. She cared for him."

"I don't believe it," Hedy objected.

"It's not a matter of belief. He told her all about his therapy…"

"Therapy?" she repeated the word slowly. "He wasn't in therapy."

"Didn't the police tell you about it?"

Neither answered me, and we sat trapped in distrust.

"He was trying to make sense of his life. Of his past. And he told Sheila all about it."

"That's gossip," Hedy said dismissively. "Just because you don't share our beliefs…"

"Neil Breuler wasn't Guy's first boyfriend."

"You're making me sick," she said. "We told you about the woman at work…"

"Maybe he was bisexual – who knows? But he was unhappy. That's why he went to a therapist."

"If you're right, he should have told us," Hedy said. "We would've helped him."

Nick had let her take over. I could feel him dreading the next word, keeping still. Too still.

"I think he wanted to, Hedy, but how could you have helped? Guy knew what you think about sex, and your guru's stance…"

"What do you know!" she cut me off.

"Sheila said as much. Guy told her."

"So you're taking her side? Has she been telling stories to the police?"

"This has nothing to do with sides."

Nick moved to stand. He must have seen they could no longer shelter each other.

"I think you should hear me out, Nick." I tried to maintain a calm front. "Guy was drawn to older men. Neil Breuler and the others were all twenty years older."

Hedy leaned forward despite herself.

"Like a father," I said.

For a moment I thought Nick was going to bang a fist on the table, but he didn't threaten me, or tell me to leave.

"You see," I continued, dreading my next words, "he told Sheila everything. And your mother knew what was wrong, too. She told me that herself. During one of his vacations Guy confided in her – that he'd been molested. He never told her who it was, but eventually he told his therapist. It took him over twenty years to admit it."

"No!" exclaimed Hedy, her face flushed.

"And his therapist urged him to keep a memory journal. I never found one the day I packed up, but it might have been on his computer."

Hedy kept shaking her head and her hair fell forward, the way it had when she was a young girl playing her cello. "We have his computer. The police gave it back to us. Nick," she looked to her husband, "did you find anything on it?" She spoke hesitantly, as if for a moment she thought there might be some proof of my allegations.

"Just his eBay records," Nick said, with a tremor in his chin.

"There," Hedy insisted. "What do you want us to do? Show you his computer?"

"The computer's not important now. But Guy's therapist also told him to stop hiding what had happened. That's why he told Sheila. He trusted her, she was safe. He knew she had troubles of her own and maybe that comforted him. But telling her wasn't enough. He had to confront the person who'd done it. You see, Guy never forgot."

"Who did this?" Hedy asked. "If you know, tell me."

For a moment I felt my stomach churn. Hadn't they already suffered enough? Nick watched me as if a stranger had suddenly appeared at his dining-room table.

"His father," I said.

Hedy yelped, like an animal caught by a trap, and covered her mouth with one hand.

"I don't know what went on between you two," I said, facing Nick. "I only know what Guy said. But your mother warned you that somebody had *touched* Guy – that was her word – and she can't understand why you cut her out of your life."

Nick slumped back in his chair.

"Guy was making it up," Hedy began to sob. "That therapist, that therapist must have brainwashed him. They do that. Everyone knows it. And it's sick. Sick. Guy must've been brainwashed."

"Guy told Sheila everything, Nick. I'm not sure of the year, but Hedy said you had some kind of breakdown in the early nineties. Anyhow, I don't know which came first, the breakdown or that camping trip when…"

"That's a lie!" Hedy said, putting up her hand, as if to block my words. Eerily, Nick didn't move.

I turned back to him. "What happened in his basement, Nick? You were there, weren't you? When he died? Can we stop pretending that you weren't there?"

Hedy's mouth fell open, and Nick's face darkened with a surge of fear, which I felt, too.

"You were there?" she asked softly, and for a moment her eyes locked with Nick's, as if she might consider the thought.

Then – at least it seemed to me – Hedy made a decision to go no further. And Nick remained silent.

"I can guess a few things. Neil Breuler had broken off with Guy, he didn't want to see him anymore. Not in the middle of a messy divorce."

My voice was the only sound in the room, leading me on.

"Maybe that left Guy frantic. Maybe he thought his new life was collapsing. Remember, Guy was really quite innocent. Did he tell you about Neil? Guy must have been in a terrible state. Maybe he was going to tell Hedy and you argued with him, and in the midst of it something went wrong…"

"That shrink put thoughts in his head," Nick finally said bitterly. "And you want to believe this rubbish."

"He confronted you…"

"Stop it," Hedy cried. "You've got to stop. Please."

"He was talking crazy, he was accusing me of things that never happened," Nick said, the muscles in his neck throbbing.

"Yet two head wounds? The coroner couldn't explain it. Guy must have been pushed with some force."

A tear rolled down Nick's cheek. Was there a look of relief in his eyes? Impossible, but that's what I saw.

"Is that true?" asked Hedy, her voice now filled with uncertainty.

"You don't understand," he replied. "He was saying crazy things, and when he backed away from me, his head cracked into the wall…"

"You were there?" Hedy repeated.

Nick turned his face from us.

"And you panicked," I continued. "But then Guy fell forward, hitting the cement floor with his forehead, and never moved again. Maybe he died at once, I don't know, I'm not a doctor. You must have thought so."

He didn't reply, and I looked back to Hedy. "You're Nick's life," I said. "The measure of it. He couldn't tell you."

She stared at me blankly.

"The next day you heard from the police, and their investigation started up. No wonder Nick thought he'd had a heart attack."

Nick didn't say a word, his hands clenched together.

"I won't listen anymore," Hedy objected, with less conviction in her voice. "You don't know what you're saying. We're always together. Nick didn't see Guy without me."

"But you go out to estate sales alone, you said so."

Hedy glanced at Nick, her eyes flashing fear. "You have to stop," she insisted breathlessly. "You're talking about my husband. I know him better than anyone. This is some horrible fantasy. It's disgusting."

I looked back at Nick. "I don't think you ever meant to harm Guy."

Without a word Nick stood, towering, and I drew back. As he walked out of the dining room I wondered if they had a gun nearby. I'd made a hell of a mess, and the best of our past had been used up.

"You fool!" Hedy exclaimed to me, and then ran after her husband. She would find a way to console him.

A door slammed off the kitchen and I followed her there.

Hedy stood in the hallway, by the door to a small bathroom. "Nick? Are you okay?"

No reply.

"Let me in," she called. "Please, let me in. I don't believe a word of it. Not a word."

We stood waiting together. "Nick!" she pounded on the door. "Nick!"

Time seemed to stop. I could feel the blood rushing in my head. "Nick," I joined her.

Then I heard the siren of a police car approaching the farmhouse. The transmitter in my cell phone had worked, just like Lieutenant Foley said it would.

The bathroom door opened slowly and Nick stood there with an empty pill bottle in each hand. He didn't look at Hedy, or at me, but down at his hands, and she reached out as he stepped forward, a dazed assent on his face. "Nick, Nick!" she said in almost a whisper.

"Let me help," I offered.

Hedy turned to me. "Get out of here!" she said with a glare of contempt. "You fool! Get out. You don't know it, but you're the one who's lost."

22

Monday, September 10

The long hot summer finally burned itself out, but nothing is ever finished – perhaps Hedy was at least right about that. You may think I'm a melancholy cynic but I've kept my promise, I've put down what I've seen, as directly as possible.

In half a year, the *dramatis personae* of my life changed completely. As a child I had no use for fairy tales and their idiotic endings, except for "The Emperor's New Clothes." Of course the emperor was naked, what else could he be? As well, there are no true endings – no finality but death – so if I bring you up to date about what happened, it's not because I believe in that thing called closure. It's because I believe in facts.

Last month I spent a week in Maine, looking at the ocean. One day it occurred to me that there might be some Yankee common sense in Emerson's famous essay about friendship, since the events of the spring and summer rarely left my thoughts. Though Emerson considered friendship a form of love, he was cautious about it: "We over-estimate the conscience of our friend. His goodness seems better than our goodness, his nature finer, his temptations less." A friend, he claimed, is a paradox of nature: "a sane man who exercises not my ingenuity, but me." *Me.* Since truth is essential to friendship, Emerson considered it "better to be a nettle in the side of your friend than his echo." Without intending to, I'd taken his advice literally. But Emerson never tried to explain what it's like to be a nettle.

How well do we ever know the people closest to us? Oh, yes, we think we do, we tell ourselves we do, perhaps we have to, out of love. But love's not enough to make us better than we are. I've seen so many people with plenty of love in their lives – devoted couples, cherished children, close families, dear friends – and they're no less selfish for all the love they've known. And what about me? I have to live with my own betrayal of friendship. Though I never risked the loss of Nick and Hedy's affection, when Lieutenant Foley suggested the cell-phone transmitter I might have ignored his prompting, no matter the reasons. This guilt is mine, along with the knowledge that I'd finally stopped thinking detachment could excuse my evasions. Maybe that's what Hedy meant when she said I was lost.

So where are we today? Like it or not, friendship has its twilight, its blue hour.

On my return home from Maine, the autumn anemones that Sheila planted last spring were already blooming, their white and lavender flowers a startling beauty, though without any lingering scent. I set Hedy's badger on the lamp table beside my reading chair. It stood for the best in her, the small creature's face looking up to me, ready to defend its young, its lair. I wanted to see Hedy like that and forget the rest.

Of course Guy's letters from Harriet Beecher Stowe never surfaced. I made several attempts to locate them with phone calls and e-mails, as did Claire Warren, but our contacts came up empty-handed. The letters might have disappeared into a private collection, or Guy's expert appraiser may have kept them for himself, or perhaps they never existed, except in Guy's imagination. Was he seeking attention with some pointless delusion? I care about preserving the past, that's been the work of my life, but, oddly enough, I don't mind. Even if the letters exist, they would change very little.

Mrs. Carney – Doris – moved in with her daughter temporarily after the shooting, but has stayed put, against Sheila's wishes; the culprits were never caught. On a good note, Sheila's antiques have surprisingly been estimated at a hundred grand, minimum, though buyers aren't standing in line. And according to Lieutenant Foley, Mrs. Roberts returned to Knoxville several days after her son's arrest, without seeing him.

By the middle of August Neil was ready to move on. He'd found a new job in Toledo, an hour west of Oberlin, in a city where his life could be a blank slate. Theo's subsequent depression frightened Daphne enough for her to intervene on her brother's behalf. He now takes a daily anti-depressant and may or may not gain twenty pounds in the year ahead. Either the pills will work or his doctor will increase the dosage. Stavro might have his fill of his fiancé's troubles and give up on her, or he'll buy her some gold bauble and go on with the marriage. And one day, years from now, I might vacation in Florida, and a fat man on the beach will call out my name. When I turn, the voice could be Theo's.

Predictably, Nick survived his overdose, and he was eventually indicted on charges of manslaughter. The papers covered it all, over and over, but I didn't read them. I already knew enough. It's likely that his lawyer will fall back on an insanity defense, though they can't count on a hung jury. Not when you've flipped the Oedipal equation. Filicide, it's called. And Guy, poor Guy, he was born in the wrong family.

Hedy will probably remain at her husband's side, or as close as the law will allow. I don't see her packing up and moving to a warmer climate. For the first time in her life she'll have to face being alone. Meditating alone. Opining alone. Now I'll never learn what she feared, or guessed. Or if she knew anything at all. Maybe she'll sculpt more raccoons, or add foxes and squirrels to her repertoire. When we last spoke, before Nick's suicide fumble, she'd mentioned ordering a new kiln.

All of these things might happen, or none of them. This ending isn't a closed one, summed up like an old-fashioned novel, but it's not an open one either, a slick modernist gesture, because endings aren't like that in life – they don't change from day to day, until we're dead. Life's not open-ended forever, although we might wish to think that. But for now, Guy's dead, Sheila's recovering, Nick's in jail, Theo refuses to answer the telephone, and with any luck, I'll never see Hedy again. Of course I'm still perplexed by friendship.

I can always get a dog or cat for company, for someone to talk to, but it hasn't come to that yet.

Acknowledgements

Special thanks to Lieutenant Mike McCloskey of the Oberlin Police Force for answering more procedural questions than he probably anticipated, and to Oberlin's Dawn Quarick, Medical Office Coordinator of the Lorain County Coroner, to Richard Riley of Ben Franklin/MindFair Books, and to Mariel L. Suffoletto of Mercy Allen Hospital, for their gracious help. Once again, thanks to Iris Gorfinkel, M.D., for her kind assistance with medical matters, and Linda Beebe, Esq., for legal concerns relating to the Revised Code of Ohio Coroners. As always, my thanks to first readers Larry Fineberg and Lee Rainey; to the next eyes, Chris Doda, Priscila Uppal and Diane Young; and, finally, to Barry Callaghan for his thoughtful notes and much-appreciated encouragement. And, of course, my appreciation to Nina Callaghan for meticulous copy-editing and to Matt Shaw for careful proofreading.

Richard Teleky, a professor in the Humanities Department of York University, in Toronto, is a critically acclaimed fiction writer, poet, and critic. His books include the novels *Winter in Hollywood*, *Pack Up the Moon*, and the award-winning *The Paris Years of Rosie Kamin*, and a collection of short fiction, *Goodnight, Sweetheart and Other Stories*; two poetry collections – *The Hermit in Arcadia* and *The Hermit's Kiss*; two non-fiction studies – *The Dog on the Bed: A Canine Alphabet*, about the human/dog bond, and *Hungarian Rhapsodies: Essays on Ethnicity, Identity, and Culture*. He is also the editor of *The Exile Book of Canadian Dog Stories* and *The Oxford Book of French-Canadian Short Stories*. His work has appeared in numerous journals in Canada and the United States, and he is a frequent contributor to *Queen's Quarterly*.